HERMAN

D0061745

HERMAN

a novel by
LARS SAABYE CHRISTENSEN

Translated by
STEVEN MICHAEL NORDBY

WHITE PINE PRESS

© 1992 Lars Saabye Christensen

Translation © 1992 Steven Nordby

All rights reserved. This book, or parts thereof,
may not be reproduced in any form without permission.

Originally published in Norway by J. W. Cappelens Forlag, Oslo.

Publication of this book was made possible, in part,
by grants from
the National Endowment for the Arts,
the New York State Council on the Arts,
Norwegian Literature Abroad (NORLA),
and the Amter Foundation.

Book design by Watershed Design.

Cover image is from Erik Gustavson's film version of Herman.

Printed in the United States of America.

ISBN 1-877727-24-5

WHITE PINE PRESS
76 Center Street Fredonia,
New York 14063

HERMAN

FALL

1.

HERMAN BENDS HIS HEAD backwards and stares up in the tree where the leaves are yellow and red and are already hanging quite loose. Between the thin, black branches he sees the sky, where the clouds move recklessly in all directions. He gets a little dizzy standing that way, as if it is he who's racing away at full speed. But it's quite pleasant too, for a while anyway, as long as he does not crash into the Monolith. He closes his eyes, but when he is about to fall down, he opens them quickly again and breathes easier. He is still in Frogner Park, has not moved so much as a centimeter.

And then he sees the first leaf flutter down. It's hanging on the end of a branch and does not appear very solid. The wind whirls it round and round, then it sails toward the fountain like a wounded bullfinch. Herman runs after it, staring at the red, restless point in the air. The wind lifts the leaf up and down. Herman spurts in zig-zags over the gravel and hopes he tied his shoelaces with double granny knots this morning. Then, it's as if the leaf, or the wind, gives up. It falls wearily toward the ground, right in front of Herman. He stops quickly, his mouth wide open and catches the leaf in his jaw, perfect as a hungry anteater.

And right then he notices that someone is spying on him; there is someone standing behind one of the statues. He can see a pink school bag just barely sticking out. He remains standing completely still. It doesn't taste very good, but he has known worse, the stiff film on chocolate pudding, for example, or the skin on milk, or the eel his father fishes for on the pier. Suddenly the school bag is gone, but he knows that someone is still standing there behind the statue of the huge lady who has at least sixteen kids hanging in her hair. And while he stands there not quite knowing what to do, he swallows the leaf. And it's very strange to think that the same leaf, a little while ago, had hung on a huge tree, and now it was down in the middle of his stomach. Maybe he could get out of eating his vegetables at dinner.

Then she comes out from behind the statue. It's Ruby. Ruby from his class. She has been standing behind the statue the entire time. Herman doesn't quite know if he especially likes that. Ruby has a mass of red hair that some claim there are five birds nests in. She holds her hands behind her back as if she has a big secret. She looks strangely at Herman with one of her eyes half-closed.

"Are you eating leaves?" Ruby asks.

"Once in awhile."

"You're the only one I know who eats leaves."

"Then you don't know many," says Herman, fetching his school bag by the bench.

Ruby follows him and takes a closer look at his face.

"Are you following me?" Herman asks.

Ruby laughs loudly and even more leaves fall from the trees.

"I've been feeding my duck carrots and hot dogs. Maybe you'll get sick. You look sick already."

"I'm healthy as a fish," says Herman. That's what Grandfather usually says, even though Grandfather lies in a canopy bed on the fourth floor and can't walk. Maybe that's why he puts it that way, healthy as a fish.

"Fish don't eat leaves," says Ruby.

"They eat worms. That's worse."

They walk together over the bridge. A drunk has slept under the *Sinnataggen** and looks just as furious. The Frogner swimming pools are empty and green and the ten meter diving board reaches all the way to the sky. Soon it starts to rain. Down by the water, the ducks swim around each other and have no bearings. A swan raises its wings, but decides not to bother and folds them together. Ruby leans over the parapet and points.

"There's my duck!"

"Your duck?"

"The one I feed."

"How can you tell the ducks apart?"

Ruby turns toward Herman, shaking her head. Her huge red hairdo bounces up and down, but at least no birds fly out of it.

"I'm not telling." But then she adds quickly: "Maybe some other time."

They walk on toward the gate without saying anything, but when they get to Kirke Road, she comes even closer and stares at his face for a very long time. Herman begins to get nervous.

"Do I look sick now?"

"Your eyes are completely green! And your nose is orange!"

With that, she runs up the street toward Majorstua. At Oscar Mathiesen she turns and waves, but Herman doesn't see it. He is already on the way to Skillebekk. And now he truly is feeling ill. Maybe he is really getting sick. Maybe his arms are turning into branches and someone will want to use them for firewood when winter comes. He feels the leaf down in his stomach, lying diagonally and tickling. His arms are already beginning to get stiff; he has to press them against his body. He sees himself in the mirror at the barber shop on Bygdøy Avenue, and it's one of those mirrors where he can see his profile too if he bends forward and turns his head. And now he really gets scared. He doesn't recognize himself. His nose is a pine cone, his ears look like two woodpecker holes, and his hair lies planted like green moss over his forehead. Herman takes off and hides in a doorway before Fats sees him. There he makes up his mind. He sticks a finger down his throat, just like Father sometimes does on Sundays. Herman sticks his finger so far down that he almost can poke the leaf. And then it comes up at full speed, along with his lunch and two caramels he found on the way to school. The leaf is still red and smells worse than gym shoes. A gust of wind carries it out into the street. It tumbles end-over-end along the gutter, where the leaf disappears between the bars of a storm drain. Herman straightens up and feels better already. It's really too bad about the caramels, he thinks, wondering if he should eat them again. He does and strolls calmly down Gabels Street. Three plus three trees is a forest, Herman says aloud. But what is one times one? It must be a very lonely forest.

It starts raining. Herman doesn't bother to run the last bit though. And when he turns onto the street, the Bottle Man opens the window on the first floor and shows his face, which is rusty colored and gaunt. It's said that Bottle Man once was the maitre'd at The King on Drammen Road but got fired because he fell in love with a Belgian princess who was visiting, or because the King discovered that he was really Swedish. The Bottle Man is either very loud-mouthed or extremely quiet. Today he is mostly quiet, and that fits in with a Monday.

"Hermanson," he whispers. "Come here."

Herman can barely hear him. He goes closer.

"Can you return some bottles for me today?"

"One has no time," whispers Herman. "Maybe tomorrow."

"Unfortunately, tomorrow is another day," the Bottle Man mumbles and closes the window gently.

Sinnataggen, which means angry little boy in Norwegian, is the title of a sculpture by Gustav Vigeland (1869-1943). Vigeland spent a large portion of his life creating 194 sculptures with more than 600 figures, many of them lifesize, for the park's 80 acres. The Monolith, which is also mentioned in the book, stands over fifty feet high and consists of 121 human figures of all **ages.**

2.

HERMAN STANDS SHIRTLESS in the bathroom and washes alongside Father. Herman's father never eats without washing himself meticulously first, not just his hands, but everything from the belt up, and especially under the arms. Even if Father is just going to gum a single slice of bread during the Request Concert, he has to go scour his upper body and change his undershirt. It gets to be a little tiring, but it's alright too, standing there bare-chested with Father, flexing muscles. Herman's arms aren't much yet, but they'll come along alright, if he stops eating leaves. Besides, the mirror hangs so high that he only sees the top of his head, while Father is so tall he almost reaches the ceiling and has to bend over when he combs his hair with the steel comb he's so proud of. Herman's father is a crane operator.

"Have you done anything crazy today?" Father asks, looking closely at the comb before sticking it in his back pocket.

"Not that I can remember," he says.

"I guess not. Otherwise I would have seen it, right?"

Father pats him on the back and they both grin. Herman leans his head back and looks up at Father, and for an instant it's almost like when he stood under the tree in Frogner Park, but no leaves fall from Father's head.

"Have you seen any angels today?" Herman asks.

"Not a single one today either," Father sighs and smears

deodorant under both arms. Afterward, Herman gets to borrow it. It stings like crazy, but maybe it has to when it smells so good. Then they hear Mother drop a plate on the floor, and that means dinner is ready. Today is Monday, and Monday is always leftovers. It's not exactly Herman's favorite dish. He always speculates on where the leftovers actually come from because he can't remember having eaten anything resembling the leftovers either Saturday or Sunday, and Herman has a nasty suspicion that Father's eels are smuggled into the mysterious soufflé. And besides, he's not particularly hungry on Mondays. Then Father always asks if he is sick, or if he doesn't want to grow anymore. On the whole, leftovers lead to quite a lot.

Herman picks at his plate, and outside it continues raining. A dirty pigeon sits on the window ledge and whistles to itself, then flies across the street and lands on a branch. Birds are lucky not to need raincoats and hats, Herman thinks. But if it rains for forty days, like in Africa, then maybe they have to use life vests and snorkels?

"Are you sick, Herman? Or don't you want to grow anymore?"

Father talks with food in his mouth and helps himself to fourths. So there probably is eel in the soufflé.

"Herman has eaten already," says Herman.

"Eaten already? Where?" asks Mother.

"At Frogner Park."

"You shouldn't eat between meals," says Father. "Then you'll just grow in width, not in height."

"It won't happen again," Herman says and looks out the window again. The pigeon is gone now, but the rain is there, straight down from the sky. God must be pretty good at swimming, Herman thinks, not to mention Jesus, who walked on water in his youth. Herman is proud that his father is a crane operator. For awhile he wondered if he should choose that way himself too, but since he gets dizzy just standing on the ground and looking up in a tree, then isn't it a little improbable that he could manage to sit at least a mile in the air and look down and at the same time lift a gigantic cable with the hook and thread it through a sewing needle in Lillestrøm?

Mother shovels the remains from Herman's plate over on hers. Mother is always the most hungry, but she is both short and thin anyway. She works at Jacobsen's Groceries on the corner. Herman likes to go there after school, and he especially likes the smell of the coffee machine behind the counter. It's odd that something that tastes so bad on the whole can smell so good.

"There was a customer who tried to rob the cash register today," Mother tells them. "He threw tomatoes and threatened us with a bunch of bananas!"

"It wasn't the Bottle Man, was it?" asks Herman.

"Of course it wasn't the Bottle Man! The Bottle Man wouldn't think of something like that."

"How much money did he take?"

"He slipped on a banana peel and ran away!"

Mother has to lay down her knife and fork while she laughs. And when Mother laughs, the trains from the West Station derail, the boat to Nesodden runs aground and the clock in the City Hall tower stops. Father draws his breath slowly and waits until it's quiet again.

"That's not the whole truth, Mom," he sighs.

"It sure is," she says. "Jacobsen Jr. called the police and reported an armed robbery. He thought the tomatoes were blood!"

"That fat-headed sissy! He runs to the police if he just loses a ballpoint pen."

"Well, he does his best."

"Yes. And that's counting pens and acting like a fool."

Herman looks from Mother to Father, thinking.

"Maybe it was Gustav Vigeland," he says.

Father lays down his knife and fork and sighs heavily several more times. Mother changes plates with Herman and suddenly bends closer, just like Ruby did, and he gets a little nervous again. Maybe he did not get up the entire leaf after all. Maybe he is about to turn into a tree without knowing it.

"You have to get a haircut tomorrow," she says.

Herman is relieved.

"Okay."

"And you haven't forgotten you're going to visit Grandfather?"

Herman shakes his head so his bangs spread out in all directions and a few strands of hair drift down on the table.

"One is not forgetful," he says.

Mother brushes away the hairs and looks at Herman again.

"I almost think you need to wear a hair net!" she laughs.

Herman laughs aloud too, but not as loudly as Mother, since he can't, while Father carries everything off from the table at once and doesn't drop so much as a toothpick on the floor.

When Herman says that he must do his lessons, he gets out of washing the dishes. So he usually says that after dinner. He goes to his room, takes out his workbook and writes: *Frogner Park by Gustav Vigeland. 58 figures on the bridge. 4 lizard figures in granite. The Rose garden. The Labyrinth. The Monolith plateau. 8 wrought iron gates. The west lawn. The Wheel of Life.* He ponders the last line. He is not completely sure, but writes anyway: *And one was agreed that it had been a nice day.* Afterward he sits there looking out the window. It's dark already. It's strange that one can see the dark, thinks Herman. But the globe is lit. It sits on the windowsill and is never turned off. He gives it a nudge, closes his eyes and stops it with his index finger. Adapazari! He erases the last sentence and writes instead: *When I grow up I am going to be a crane operator or travel to Adapazari!*

Before he goes to bed, they listen to the Request Concert. But none of them has a birthday today, so they get no greetings. Herman thinks the hymns sound sad and hopes that no one will think of sending him *The Great White Flock* when it's his turn. While Eddie Calvert plays trumpet for a soldier in Bardufoss, Father goes to the bathroom, and they know he is already hungry again.

"About time to set sail," says Mother, looking up from her game of solitaire. "And the captain has to be on board, right?"

"Land ho-ho!" says Herman and marches to the bathroom where Father stands with his shirt off, shaving. His beard grows out three times a day and five times on Sundays. Herman climbs up his back, but when he comes to the shoulders and can see in the mirror, he gets dizzy again and glides gently down. Father laughs and sticks his head under the faucet. Herman folds the toothpaste tube eighteen times and squeezes as hard as he can, and a little white clump comes out. It's really strange how toothpaste tubes never get empty.

"Time to say good night," says Herman.

"Good night," gurgles Father.

When he has gone to bed, Mother comes in and turns out the light, but the globe gets to stay on. Then she sits by the bed and strokes Herman's hair, pulls it a little, and that's something Herman likes. She usually does this when his hair gets too long and he's going to go to the barber. He decides not to get too much cut off, then he'll have to go back to the barber again soon, and Mother will stroke her hand through his hair, pull it and laugh loudly.

She closes the door carefully and Herman suddenly thinks about Ruby, all that red hair of hers. It's not entirely impossible that there are birds in it, maybe a bullfinch or a hummingbird at least. And he has to think about the leaf he swallowed. It was amazing. He will think better of it before he does something like that again. Then he hears the wind outside. It's singing a strange melody this evening. It sneaks around the corner with accordion and tight trumpets. But he has never seen the wind's face. Soon he hears Mother and Father in the living room. Fortunately, they have faces. It's too bad about time, Herman thinks. Everyone wants to take it and once in awhile kill it. Later he dreams much he cannot remember. It's really a bit annoying.

3.

HERMAN HAS FIGURED OUT that it is eight hundred and forty-two steps to school. But that's when he walks alone and not blinded and without a rain hat. When he walks with Father up to Drammen Road, he uses just eight hundred and sixteen steps because Father has such unusually long legs, and Herman must lengthen his stride as far as he can to keep up. Jacobsen's Groceries doesn't open until nine, so Mother usually stands in the window and waves to them—with both hands. And when they've gone a ways up the street, they hear her calling, and then she tosses out the lunch bag that Herman always forgets. Herman's mother is a very good thrower. Once she threw his lunch to him after he had gotten all the way to Bygdøy Avenue, and it's no less than one hundred and thirty steps there, and Herman only needed to flip open his school bag, and there landed two sandwiches with goat cheese and two with bologna right between his pencil box and his science book.

They stop at the corner by Jacobsen's. Father is going down Munkedams Road to the construction site at Vika. Herman is going straight ahead. Father leans over him and his breath smells of cigarettes and coffee.

"Someday you can go up in the crane with me," he says.

Herman looks away.

"Sure. Can you see all the way to America up there?"

"America! Even farther! I can see so far that I see my own back!"

"That's a long way," says Herman.

"That's not true," says Father quietly. "I can see to Nesodden. One shouldn't lie and make things up, right?"

"Rather not."

Father suddenly straightens up, digs in his back pocket and pulls out the steel comb.

"It's yours now," he says ceremoniously. "Use it wisely."

Herman takes the comb carefully. It shines in his hand and is good to hold.

"But what will you use?" he asks.

"I just stick my head out of the crane and the wind is my comb," says Father, and then he takes huge strides across Munkedams Road and disappears behind a flock of pigeons which suddenly alights.

Outside the Red Cross is an ambulance with huge mirrors on each side. Herman bends over and sees his face, and is amazed again, as if his whole face is just one big nose, but at least it doesn't look like a pine cone anymore. He draws the comb through his hair. It scrapes against his scalp and hurts, but maybe that is the intention, that it has to hurt if your hair is to look good. Suddenly Herman discovers that there is someone lying inside the ambulance, an ancient man with eyes of glass who doesn't blink at all. The mouth is just an open hole with teeth, and his skin is as blue and tight as a speed skater's suit. Herman jumps away and runs up the street a ways and has to think about Grandfather in his canopy bed. And now he has lost count so he may as well walk blindly. His record is twenty-six steps, but that was made in the middle of a field last summer. He closes his eyes and counts to himself. Eight. This is going well. Fifteen. This is still going very well. But when he comes to twenty-two, it's full stop. He runs into something soft that screams. Herman opens his eyes and stares right into the eyes of a fox. Further up is someone with blue hair who speaks.

"Watch where you're going, you little brat!"

Herman looks in the opposite direction and feels his way

forward with his hands.

"I'm no brat. I'm blind and have lost my way."

Herman staggers out on Bygdøy Avenue with both arms in front of him. Three cars slam on the brakes, and a bus almost parks inside Møllhausen's Bakery. Herman slips around the corner at Langbrecke, and far away he hears the school bell.

The schoolyard is completely empty, like the door is a huge vacuum cleaner. Not a lunch bag is left behind. Herman sneaks along the fence and wonders what he should say this time. And everything is very still. Maybe everyone is dead and he has escaped, thinks Herman. But when he gets inside the corridor, he hears the singing of hymns from the classrooms, and it is almost gloomy, very sad at least, almost even sadder than the Request Concert when those over a hundred get a passing greeting. He hangs his corduroy jacket on the hook, waits until they are finished singing, then he knocks and opens the door before the teacher can answer. Barrel stands behind the teacher's desk and stares at him. He has a face full of chalk already and is holding the pointer like a fencing foil. By the window sits Ruby. It looks as if she is about to laugh herself to death. Barrel takes a step toward him, and Barrel is huge, the biggest teacher in the school. He's as wide as he is tall, and he's very tall. There's a rumor that he held a seventh grader out the window by the ear on the top floor for forty minutes, but it must have been before the war.

"And what kind of excuse do you have today, Herman Fulkt?"

He can't say that he suddenly became blind and got lost in Old Town because he has said that before.

"I had to save an old lady who was attacked by a fox," says Herman.

Barrel comes even closer. He's holding the pointer with both hands now. It must be about to break. His fists are as huge as cauliflowers. Herman wonders what that guy had done to get hung out the window by the ear. His stomach starts getting a little queasy.

"A fox, huh. And where was it this fox popped up?"

"It popped up right on Bygdøy Avenue."

"I see. On Bygdøy Avenue. Maybe you can tell us how you vanquished this wild beast?"

The laughter spreads slowly in the class, from desk to desk. Ruby almost can't hold back now. That's something Herman has always wondered about, if laughter really is a sickness, because Mother always says that laughter is contagious.

"When I stepped in, the fox was already dead. It was hanging around the lady's neck and was poisoned. Can I go to the bathroom?"

Now the laughter has infected everyone. They sit with big openings in their faces that assorted sounds come out of. Some are so sick that they have to pound their desk tops. But Barrel is still healthy. He gets eight perpendicular wrinkles in his forehead and the chalk sprinkles down his cheeks.

"Sit down," he says wearily. "If you can hold it that long."

"I'll be okay," says Herman. "The bell will ring soon anyway."

Barrel gets three extra wrinkles, and Herman hurries over to the window row. He has a view of the church, and he has always wondered which is higher, the steeple, with its gilded copper spire, or his father's crane. He bets the crane. How else would they be able to build the steeple? Two desks in front of him sits Ruby, and when the light from outside shines on her hair, it's like it is on fire, just like when the sun hits the copper steeple and the whole tower glows. But today it's so overcast that even the birds must stand in line. Ruby's hair is just as nice anyway. Herman likes that she sits in front of him. The troublemakers sit farthest back, Glenn, Bjørnar and Karsten. They've already beaten up a seventh grader, stopped up the john and smoked half a pack of Cooley's. It's not very safe to have them behind you, if you don't have eyes in the back of your head. Suddenly Ruby turns around and sticks out her tongue. It almost looks like a red leaf. Herman has to laugh out loud. Barrel already has him in his binoculars, lifts the pointer and blows chalk off his nose.

"To the blackboard!"

Herman walks softly between the desks. He wonders what Barrel is going to ask about today, how tall the Monolith is, how many stomachs cows have and what they're for, or about the spruce's way from forest to furniture. Herman feels himself becoming smaller and smaller. Soon he won't reach to his own knees. When he gets up by the teacher's desk, he is so small that he can see himself in Barrel's right shoe, and it occurs to him that today he is going to get a haircut.

Herman gets a piece of chalk in his hand. It's as big as a log, and how is he going to reach up to the blackboard? It doesn't smell very good down there by Barrel's feet. Perhaps he has to draw Africa, or the whole Eidsvold building with the flag flying high, or maybe he will have to hang out of the window by the left ear? In any case, it's a good thing their classroom is on the first floor.

"Write an i with a dot over it!" says Barrel.

He is in luck. Herman immediately grows at least three feet, meets the blackboard with the chalk, draws a splendid i, and fills in a solid dot.

"And what is this?"

"An i with a dot over it," says Herman, satisfied.

"Are you lying?"

Herman becomes greatly confused, looks from the blackboard to the teacher and back again. Barrel bends over him like an overfed question mark.

"I asked you to write an i with a dot over it. Do you remember?"

"One is not forgetful."

"Are you impudent!"

"I'm Herman Fulkt."

Barrel seems to give up, takes the chalk from him and leans heavily against the blackboard where he draws yet another dot over the i.

"When I ask you to write an i with a dot over it, there should be two dots! Don't forget it!"

"Yes, sir."

Herman shuffles back to his desk, but before he gets that far, Ruby sticks a piece of paper in his hand. He unfolds it carefully when he has sat down and reads diagonally: "Do you like red hair? Hi, Ruby."

The bell rings as he's about to write a letter back, and then it's too late. Ruby is going to Homemaking and Herman is going to have Shop down in the basement. He will have to send it air mail tomorrow, or maybe by carrier pigeon, if he manages to catch one at Olaf Bull's square.

The smell of glue is so strong in the shop that Herman almost gets dizzy. The glue is in big pails by the radiator and looks like rotten jelly. Herman is in the process of making a herbarium, and he's already looking forward to spring so he can go out to Bygdøy and pick white anemones, and at Nesodden maybe he'll find bluebells and forget-me-nots. Woody still hasn't shown up. He always comes late to class. He must be sitting in the coat room, gossiping with the cleaning lady.

Suddenly Glenn, Bjørnar and Karsten are standing around him.

"Why don't you have Homemaking with the girls?" asks Glenn.

Herman tries to raise his eyes, but they are so incredibly heavy he needs a crane to get them up.

"Then you could crochet potholders and wipe your butt!" continues Karsten.

"What's the note?" asks Bjørnar.

"What note?"

Herman is not particularly good at lying. It's just as if his lower lip falls down and becomes huge as a shopping bag.

"The note from Ruby, you retard!"

"I didn't get any note from Ruby."

His lower lip becomes bigger and bigger. Soon he'll need a crutch to hold it up.

"Don't lie," says Glenn, coming closer. Glenn has hair over his forehead and braces on his teeth and claims he can chew glass.

"Note? Oh, that note, yes. A shopping list for Mom."

Now his lip is huge as a bathtub. It's almost impossible to hold his head up.

"Let's search him!" calls Karsten.

In the course of zero-point-zero, each and every pocket is turned inside out. Bjørnar holds up the steel comb, Karsten waves a fiver and Glenn has found the note.

"'Do you like red hair? Hi, Ruby,'" he howls just before his retainer pops out.

And then there is laughter again, and everyone is infected, and they are sick for a long time, and Woody still hasn't come. That laughter is worse than the measles and chicken pox put together, thinks Herman. But suddenly everyone is well again. Glenn holds his arm tightly.

"Do you like red hair, Herman?"

Herman looks down at his shoes and breathes heavily. Bjørnar sticks the steel comb like a pistol between his eyes.

"Do you like red hair!"

"I hate it," says Herman, and his lower lip glides along the floor and nasty animals climb in his mouth that he cannot manage to spit out.

"Say that Ruby is ugly!"

"Ruby is ugly."

"Say that Ruby has birds' nests in her hair!"

Herman fiddles with the herbarium which still isn't finished, and the inside of his head itches.

"Ruby has birds' nests in her hair."

Glenn lets go of Herman, and Karsten gets behind him.

"Now you're going to die!"

"Now I'm going to die," Herman repeats.

"What's your last request?"

"To have my comb back."

Bjørnar sneers and lays the steel comb in the herbarium. Karsten keeps watch at the door, and Glenn puts a piece of cardboard under Herman's sweater. And then Bjørnar sticks a knife in it so it stands out of his chest.

"He's coming!" whispers Karsten.

"Lie down! You're dead!"

Herman lies down between the benches and closes his eyes. Right away Woody is there. Woody is thin like a stalk of rhubarb and has huge transparent ears. When it's gusty he must have to hold them tight with a rubber band in order not to be blown away by the wind. He stands there, looking around, surprised because everyone is completely still, and Woody is not exactly used to that. Then he catches sight of Herman. Woody has to hold the door frame tightly, then he storms through the room, knocks over two pails of glue, waves his arms and screams. He falls down next to Herman, is about to pull out the knife, but doesn't dare touch it. Herman lies completely still and senses that Woody smells of perfume, or maybe it's just the glue.

"What happened!" Woody howls.

No one answers. Woody bends over him again, and Herman wants to sneeze, but maybe it's not wise to sneeze when you have a knife in the heart.

"Herman, can you hear me? This is Fredrik Juell Johansen. Can you hear me, Herman?"

Herman hears him very well, but doesn't quite know if he should answer. It might be best to wait a little, until Woody calms down.

"Get the nurse!" he screams. "Get the nurse!"

But no one moves and no one says anything. Woody takes Herman's hand and lays his huge ear to his mouth. It tickles.

"Herman...Herman...Don't move...Help is on the way...You're going to be alright...Take it easy...Herman ...How are you?"

Herman opens his eyes and looks right into Woody's ear. It looks like the inside of a huge mussel.

"One is fine, thank you."

Woody's face tightens. He looks around confused while everyone stares another way and begins whistling *Bridge On the River Kwai.* Herman slowly rises and goes over to his bench, pulls out the knife, and the piece of cardboard falls on the floor.

Then no one can whistle cleanly. Laughter pours out of

their faces and makes the walls bulge. But suddenly no one is laughing any longer. They can hear another sound that frightens them, that confuses them. Woody is on his knees on the floor, and he's crying. He doesn't try to hide it. His hands hang perpendicular along his dusty coat, and he cries.

On the way home, Herman has almost forgotten about going to the barber. He wants most of all to take a boat to Australia, or at least the Frogner Streetcar all the way to Disen. On Skov Road he sees the lady who almost can't walk because she has fleas in her legs. He has heard of people with ants in their pants, but this must be worse. She uses two crutches and teeters away while her whole body shakes. Herman wonders how the fleas managed to get into her legs. Maybe she happened to swallow them by accident? She looks extremely sad, and Herman usually crosses the street when he sees her.

On Bygdøy Avenue, chestnuts slam to the asphalt, and he gathers up a load and puts them in his school bag. They can be handy, especially in the winter. Then he goes in the barber's.

It's really very nice to be with Fats. Fats always has wet hair and a narrow, black mustache. The best thing is when he steps on the pedal and the chair gets higher and higher; it's probably the closest Herman comes to a crane operator. And it's nice to see the combs in blue water and the posters for Brylcreem and Cheseline, with pictures of sweethearts who have wavy hair and nice faces.

"And how do you want it today?" asks Fats when he has finished stepping on the pedal and already has to wipe off the sweat.

"I think I want it like my brother's."

"And how is your brother's?"

"I don't have a brother!"

Both laugh a long while, and Fats drops a pair of scissors, laces his fingers into Herman's hair and begins clipping while he sings a familiar melody from the Request Concert. Fortunately it isn't a hymn.

It's really strange to look in the mirror, because on the wall behind him is another mirror. That's where the ladies sit with astronaut helmets. Herman can see himself in the barber chair in hundreds of rooms that become smaller and smaller and disappear in a point no bigger than a fly. There are remarkable things at the barber's. He also has footrests and tissue paper that sticks around the throat and a huge bib that is soon covered with blond hair. Maybe he should become a barber? Better than a shop teacher.

Suddenly Fats stops clipping. Herman bends his head backward and looks up in his nostrils, and there must be room for eight chestnuts in each of them. Fats pushes his head back in place, wrestles with the scissors, but then he looks down at Herman's scalp again. Herman often wonders who cuts Fats' hair, or who pulls the dentist's teeth and who cuts out the doctor's appendix. But it's strange how long Fats stands there staring. Herman starts to get anxious. Maybe he has clipped so much that he can see his thoughts? That wouldn't have been very good.

Finally Fats straightens up, fishes out a wet comb and splits his hair in a straight part.

"Shall we call that good, Herman?"

"Yes, I think we shall."

"Can you tell your mother I'd like to talk with her?"

"She just got a permant."

"That's permanent, Herman. I want to talk with her anyway."

"Alright, Fats."

And then comes the very finest, when he brushes away the hair from his neck with the soft brush made out of llama tails from inner Peru.

Herman gets two crowns back from the five, puts the money in his pocket and goes out. The wind is cold against his slicked down hair. And suddenly a chestnut crashes straight down on his skull. It almost embeds itself. He must shake it loose and feels wet hair flicker across his face. Then he just takes out the steel comb, gets in front of the three section mirror in the window and combs his hair in place again. At the same time, Fats' face comes into view. He peeks out from behind the mirror and sees Herman, and Fats has one of those sad colors in his eyes, almost as sad as the Lady with the Fleas. He probably needs cheering up, so Herman holds out the comb so Fats can see it up close, because he is quite curious too. Fats tries to smile, but it's not a complete success.

Herman sticks the comb in his back pocket and sprints across Bygdøy Avenue.

At Jacobsen's Groceries, Mother stands behind the counter and looks completely different than at home. She has a white apron on, and she has a net over her hair that looks like a spider web. At the cash register sits Jacobsen Jr. himself, who everyone says resembles a famous American movie star. He has dark hair in back and a cleft chin, but almost never smiles, only when there is a large total to do. And he has quite a few ballpoint pens in his breast pocket.

First, Herman must go over to the coffee machine. He closes his eyes while he sniffs in all he can. If he could remember his dreams, they would surely smell like that.

Mother stands next to him and has a pencil behind her ear.

"Your hair looks nice," she says.

"Thank you for offering."

Jacobsen Jr. punches in a sum on the cash register, clears his throat loudly and looks around. He must have sold at least a couple of pounds of ground meat, or maybe a chop. When someone just buys flatbread and salt, he doesn't clear his throat at all. Not to mention bottle deposits. Then he leaves the shop and goes out to the back room where there is a radio and foreign magazines.

"Have you been attacked today?" asks Herman.

"Today there was just a dog that peed on the cauliflower. We have to sell them for half-price."

"What are we having for dinner?"

"Pish fudding and topedos."

"With chocolate sauce?"

"Of course! Haven't you forgotten Grandfather?"

"Grandfather's not forgotten."

Mother sets out a cardboard box on the counter, and Herman knows exactly what's in it: Six green apples, eight carrots, five fish cakes, a bottle of milk and two slabs of chocolate. Grandfather is healthy as a fish.

"Fats wants to talk with you."

"With me? Why?"

"He wants to cut your pergamet."

"You're pulling my leg again, Herman."

"No, I'm not. Fats wants to talk to you."

Mother places the box in his arms and pushes him toward the door just as the Bottle Man comes in, and Jacobsen Jr. gets up and disappears out to the back room. The Bottle Man has two bags full of empty bottles, and he shakes so much that it sounds like a drum corp three weeks before Independence Day.

"Do you have fleas in your legs too?" asks Herman.

The Bottle Man's knees give way at the same time. He sinks down on the floor and lies there in a pile of bottles. People are acting unusually strange today, thinks Herman, and hurries out. He can hear the Bottle Man yelling inside.

"I do not have fleas! I do not have fleas! Take them away! Take them away!"

And Mother's voice:

"Of course not, Frantsén. Now let's count your bottles and figure out how much it is today.

Fortunately, it isn't far to Grandfather's, across the streetcar tracks, past the hot dog stand, and almost down to the trains. But Grandfather lives on the fourth floor, and that's a lot of stairs when one is almost without legs. Herman has decided to buy an elevator for Grandfather someday when he can afford it.

The door on the top floor is always open, and Herman goes in. First there is a narrow entry where photographs hang on the wall. One of the pictures shows Herman's mother and father on a boat that is just about to capsize. They were much younger then, and Herman doesn't quite know if he likes that picture. Another photograph is of himself. He is sitting in the middle of a big, ugly bathtub, screaming, and his head is as shiny as a blue balloon. He can't remember ever looking like that. It must be a mix up.

In the next room Grandfather lies in a bed with a red canopy sky. He has been there since Grandmother died. She died before Herman was born. Grandfather's legs are thin as pencils, and they have already taken their last steps, as Mother usually says on Saturdays. But he lies pretty well at least. It doesn't smell particularly great at Grandfather's. Herman opens the window, then he sets the groceries on the night table which is also a day table. The first thing Grandfather does is drink milk right from the bottle. Herman goes out to the bathroom and empties the pot. When he comes back, Grandfather has already eaten four fish cakes and looks happy. And in the corner the old grandfather clock is ticking, just like always.

"Do we have time to talk today?" he whispers and lays his strange hand on Herman's arm.

"I have a roast in the oven."

That's what Mother usually says when salesmen or Mormons come to the door. Grandfather chuckles a long time. Such a canopy bed is quite nice. Maybe you remember all your dreams in it.

"What have you done today, Herman?"

"I lied today. Several times."

"That's not very good. But tomorrow you'll tell the truth."

"Don't know if I'm strong enough for that."

"Don't come up with excuses."

"Excuse me."

"Why did you lie?"

"Glenn and Karsten and Bjørnar forced me. They stuck a knife in my heart so I was lying dead on the floor."

"Well that changes everything," says Grandfather. "I remember I lied once. It was in Turkey during the war. They pulled out eight nails and then I talked. That doesn't count."

Grandfather is completely bald except for three hairs by each ear. It's not much to brag about. And they're just about to fall out too. His skull is bumpy as a granite boulder and has almost the same color. But he can't see Grandfather's thoughts, and Herman is glad about that. He often wonders if he is the same way underneath his hair. It's not easy to tell. Grandfather is probably the oldest person in the world. It's truly a strange thing that both newborns and old people have almost no hair.

"Have I told you about the time I fell off a ladder with a bucket of paint in each hand?"

"You were going to paint the window frames on the second floor at Nesodden."

"Fortunately there was grass where I fell. But I got the paint all over me and was quite green. This was around midsummer, and they didn't find me until the end of August. Do you want the last fish cake?"

"I shouldn't eat between meals."

"Then I'll take it. But otherwise, I was healthy as a fish. What are you looking at, Herman?"

"Your head. Why don't you have any hair?"

"Because I'm going to die soon. It's just like fall. The leaves falling."

"Do you become winter in the end, then?"

"Yes. A long, long winter."

When Herman comes home, he hears Mother drop two plates on the floor, and that's nothing unusual. Father stands in the bathroom with a towel over his shoulder and stares at him, as if they have never seen each other before.

"Hello Herman," Father finally says, but his voice is different, as if he's speaking into an empty flower pot.

Herman realizes it now. Father must have seen everything from up in the crane, that he told dirty lies about Ruby.

"It wasn't on purpose," he mumbles.

"What wasn't on purpose?" asks Father quietly.

"You saw me, didn't you?"

Father has to think about it thoroughly, wraps his head in the towel. Then he peeks out again.

"I haven't seen you all day. There were too many clouds.

But I helped an airplane that was going to Fornebo."

He throws the towel over to Herman.

"That's not the whole truth," continues Father. "I didn't see a single plane. Just a bird. Gave it a piece of bread."

Mother comes into view with tired eyes and soot on her face.

"You can skip washing up. Dinner's ready."

"But you have to wash up," laughs Herman and tosses the towel to Mother.

The fish pudding is rather scorched and the potatoes are almost sauce. Herman regrets not eating between meals with Grandfather. Mother is not especially hungry either. She talks the whole time about the Bottle Man, who claimed that the beer bottles were full of fleas, and Jacobsen Jr., who got a visit from a lady with a big hat and long skirt.

"Are you sick, Mother?" Herman asks.

She turns quickly toward him and looks odd.

"Sick? Why do you ask that?"

"You're eating so little."

"She's on a diet again," says Father.

Mother looks up, helps herself to a burned slice of fish pudding and talks with her mouth full.

"Maybe you think I'm too fat?"

"I can lift you with one finger," boasts Father, but fortunately he doesn't do it right there.

"Maybe you can lift Grandfather down to the ground with the crane," suggests Herman.

"Now that's an idea. But it must be carefully planned."

"We'll take him out through the window. But we have to do it before winter comes."

"How was Grandfather?" asks Mother.

"He's healthy as a fish."

Father gets up and clears the table, but drops a fork on the floor, and when he goes to pick it up, a glass falls too.

"Did you talk with Fats?" asks Herman, looking at Mother, since he almost doesn't dare look at Father. He is crawling around on the linoleum and picking up shards of glass, and his neck is quite red.

"Oh, yes. I talked with Fats. Where's the change?"

"I thought you'd forgotten," laughs Herman.

"Well, I did forget," Mother says. "Buy yourself anything you want."

Herman looks at her, confused.

"But can we afford it?"

"It's alright, Herman."

Father rises suddenly and almost butts his head into the ceiling.

"I talked to the foreman, not that I needed to talk to the foreman, but you can come up in the crane with me one of these days. What do you say to that?"

Herman does not quite know what he should say to that. But he doesn't want to disappoint Father.

"That will be fine. Then I can see my own back."

Father tosses the glass bits in the dust bin and sits down quickly.

"And then we'll go fishing for eel!"

Herman looks away. Father bends over the table and swings his arms to show his strength.

"At Fred Olsen Wharf! That's where the best ones are. That's because the sewer comes out right there."

"Stop it!" yells Mother, rising with a start.

Father looks around in distress. Herman knows he needs help.

"But I'd rather not strangle them," he says.

Father smiles, relieved.

"We won't strangle them, Herman. We'll use nails. In the noggin. Right into the brain. Like this!"

Mother is already fleeing the room.

The evening becomes stranger and stranger. Father eats dinner without washing, and Mother takes out a cap she began knitting last year. Herman figures that maybe it's best to say good night right away, and then he takes all the chestnuts up to bed with him. It's one of his favorite things, opening chestnuts. That something so nice and smooth can be found inside such a shell with spiny burs is almost unbelievable. He lays the chestnuts next to him on the pillow, and once in awhile he has to put one of them in his mouth.

Just then Mother comes in and sits down silently by the bed.

"Are you eating chestnuts, Herman?"

"Umph tastessing."

Mother strokes her finger along the part in his hair. He begins to laugh and has to spit out the chestnut. It hits the globe in the middle of America.

"Your hair really looks nice."

"Not so bad."

"Have you done your homework?"

"No, and that's final."

"It doesn't matter. You're not going to school tomorrow. We're going to take a trip to the doctor."

Herman sits up in bed and is wide awake.

"Are you sick, Mother?"

She lays her finger on his forehead and pushes him slowly down in the bed again.

"The doctor just wants to take a peek at us. It's nothing serious."

Whenever she talks like that, Herman gets even more nervous.

"It's not appendicitis, is it?" he asks.

"Do you have a stomachache?"

"Maybe. But I didn't mean to eat that leaf."

"Did you eat a leaf, Herman?"

"Between meals in Frogner Park. It fell right down in my mouth."

"Didn't you spit it out?"

"Afterward. Did you eat a leaf too, Mother?"

"I ate tree sap once. But that was a long time ago. Before you were born."

"We'll be alright," says Herman.

Mother strokes him through the hair, and afterward she must examine her fingers. It's strange how she keeps acting. Herman closes his eyes and pretends he's sleeping. But when she has turned out the light and closed the door, he gets up, goes over to the window and peeks out under the shade. In his hand he holds a chestnut. The globe shines with a dark yellow light, and in the black sky is the moon, white and round. Maybe the moon is the wind's eye, thinks Herman. Then the wind must be a pirate with a patch over the other eye.

He crawls far under the comforter and worries about going with his mother to the doctor. It always smells dangerous at the doctor's. But at least he gets out of going to school tomorrow. Maybe Mother's luck is sick, because she sometimes says she has ill luck. Herman hears her talking softly in the living room as if she has a secret. And after awhile he can also hear Father fetching the bottle that sits on the top shelf of the pantry, even though it's only Tuesday. Maybe he has to stick his finger in his throat on Wednesdays now.

Right before he falls asleep, Herman decides that he is going to remember his dreams tonight. But all he remembers afterward is the moon, Grandfather's skull and the chestnuts. And there is no dream.

4.

WHEN MOTHER WAKES HIM, he still has the chestnuts in his hand. But the moon has slid down from the sky and Father has long since gone to the construction site. It's past ten o'clock. Herman hasn't slept so late on a Wednesday since the summer he learned to swim and got the chicken pox. Mother has a blue dress with white dots on, and she brings him breakfast in bed—a piece of toast with rindless orange marmalade and tea directly from India. She doesn't look particularly ill. In any case she doesn't seem to be running out of time. But then she gets a big glass of water and asks Herman to drink it slowly.

"The doctor is going to want a pee sample," she says. "Try to hold it until we get there."

"What does he want it for?"

"Everyone who goes to the doctor has to pee."

Herman drinks half the glass and gives the rest to Mother.

"You'd better drink some too."

Mother empties the glass in four swallows and afterward she watches him closely while he washes. And he has to put on the gray trousers that pinch and the shirt that he usually wears on Independence Day and Christmas Eve. It has gotten tighter since last time. It's good to know. At last Mother stands behind him and combs his hair with her own brush, which looks like a dried out porcupine. Herman pulls out the steel comb, but then her face becomes strange again and she backs him out in the hall where his corduroy jacket is hanging ready.

"Guess what we're having for dinner today!" she says quickly.

"Beatmalls and rarcots?"

"No!"

"Awffles and uitfray?"

"No!"

"Then I give up."

"Chicken!"

Herman thinks about that chicken almost the entire way to the doctor. There's a lot that can happen on such a Wednesday. He holds Mother's hand; she has on smooth gloves and is wearing a hat. On Bygdøy Avenue, the chestnuts continue to fall like green bombs. The trees suddenly look so tired. They will be naked soon, certainly freezing where they stand, all in a row. Herman forgets the chicken for awhile and thinks about Grandfather. Is he freezing too? Is he freezing in his canopy bed?

The doctor's office is right next to the Frogner Theater. *Zorro* is playing this week.

"Maybe Father will take you to the five o'clock show Saturday," says Mother.

"Maybe?"

"I'm sure of it!"

Herman gets so distracted by all this that he must pretend he's a horse. He gallops down the sidewalk and breathes heavily through the nose and Zorro nearly hops down from the billboard and rides along. But when they get to the entrance and begin climbing the crooked stair steps, he forgets both Zorro and the chicken, and neither is Mother standing tall, as Father says after he's been to sports competitions against Sweden. It smells worse than anything, old appendices, amputated feet in formaldehyde, frost bite and needle stabs. Herman suddenly stops and pushes his face into Mother's coat.

"Oh, Herman. What is it?"

"I don't want to!"

"It's not going to hurt. The doctor's just going to take a peek at us. Do you know what we're having for dessert?"

Herman comes out of the coat, peeks up at Mother and gets a little dizzy, because now she is standing tall again. It's sad actually, never to be able to be a crane operator.

"Maybe nogegg," he suggests.

"No!"

"Canpakes?"

"No!"

"Then I give up at once."

"Ice cream!"

This must be carefully planned. He must not eat too much chicken, or he won't be able to eat enough ice cream. He takes Mother's hand and holds her tight.

"Don't be afraid, Mother. It will be alright."

She opens the door to the waiting room, and Herman loses everything resembling appetite. It hadn't helped at all to promise rewards. Inside, very sick people sit on flimsy chairs staring right into grungy-green walls, twisting their fingers until they burn. Mother finds room for them in the corner, and it is as quiet as the grave, as Grandfather says when he talks about Grandmother. Next to Herman sits a sad, almost headless man. A lady with only one arm and a moustache smears lipstick on her mouth and misses every time. And in the middle of the floor stands a streetcar conductor who has lost a finger at Majorstua. The walls are full of posters of fat nurses displaying huge syringes and bottles of cod-liver oil that are bigger than the Monolith. Herman has to cover his eyes, but he looks between his fingers anyway. Suddenly the door opens and a policeman hobbles out. Surely he was able to walk just fine when he came in. Herman puts his face in Mother's lap and pretends to be dreaming, but this dream he absolutely does not want to remember.

It is suddenly quiet, even quieter than the grave. It is so quiet that they can hear the time ticking in a lady's wrist watch in Tokyo. Herman needs to take a peek. He lifts one eye and sees the doctor standing in the doorway playing eenee, meenee, minee, mo. Everyone in the waiting room looks away, and now it's so quiet they can hear a shiny apple fall to the grass all the way out on Nesodden. But soon there is a great noise. The doctor takes out a bed sheet and blows his nose until it shines, while he shouts to drown himself out:

"Fulkt next!"

Mother has to drag him into the examination room. The door is closed, and there is no way back. In the nearest corner stands a nurse who coughs the whole time and tries to smile simultaneously. It's difficult. In the next corner is a cabinet with bandages and newly sharpened swords. In the third corner is a mattress wrapped in paper. In the last corner is Herman. He doesn't stand very stably. The only thing nice to look at is the green plant on the windowsill which tumbles out of the flowerpot like a palm without a trunk. But everywhere it stinks to high heaven. That must be why the nurse coughs and the doctor blows his nose. Now he bends down toward Herman, who can see himself in the huge, polished tip of the doctor's nose, and the face looks strange, like a fish that wants out of an aquarium. Herman is a little bewildered. Maybe he isn't as healthy as a fish after all?

The voice above the white coat begins to speak.

"How are we today?" it asks.

"We are not completely fine," whispers Herman, looking up at Mother, who is wringing her hands as if she is also confined in an aquarium.

"And how old are you?"

The doctor is speaking strangely, as if he mistakes Herman for a poodle.

"I think I may have lost count, but I have another birthday next year too."

The doctor laughs loudly and has to hide in his handkerchief again.

"I can never remember my telephone number," he blows.

"It doesn't matter. We don't have a telephone."

Mother turns red and the doctor must laugh just as loudly again. Then he comes even closer. He smells of cough drops.

"Why don't you sit down, then I can take a little peek at

you?"

"Peek here."

"Yes, indeed."

"And no needles!"

"Agreed."

Herman pulls Mother closer.

"He wants to look at me first. Maybe it's contagious."

Mother looks at him confused, is going to say something, but gives up with a sigh that makes Herman's hair rise. He realizes that she is dreading her turn, and he wants to remind her of the chicken and dessert, but by then she's already busy taking off his shirt and undershirt. The doctor puts a cold thingamajig on his back and asks him to breath deeply in and out. It goes just fine. Mother stands next to him and smiles, but there seems to be something wrong with her smile, as if it's made of rubber bands.

The doctor stands up and pulls the plugs out of his ears.

"Am I going to die soon?" Herman asks.

"Don't talk like that!" Mother shouts.

"You are certainly healthy as a fish," the doctor smiles and blows his nose.

"That's what Grandfather says too, but soon it'll be winter."

Mother has to sit down, and the doctor becomes a little confused behind his handkerchief.

"Winter? You'll probably go skiing then?"

Herman doesn't bother answering. He's freezing. It's no wonder they caught colds in here. The doctor has pulled out a magnifying glass, puts his fingers in Herman's hair and leans over his scalp. It takes a long time. It's unbelievable how curious everyone is these days. And it is quiet again. It's so quiet that he can hear Barrel snap a piece of chalk in third period. Finally the doctor finishes, turns away and sneezes a hurricane.

"Do I have lice?" Herman asks.

"Of course not," says Mother. "How can you think of something like that?"

"Bjørnar had them last year. Six-hundred and thirty-two of them."

The nurse, who has also begun sneezing now, gives him a glass that is narrow at the bottom and big at the top.

"Now we'll just take a little pee sample. I hope you've saved some?"

"We've saved a long time."

Herman turns his back, opens up and aims. And then it comes. There is a lot. It rises and rises, and soon it almost reaches the top edge. His shoulders begin to shake.

"You're about done, aren't you?" Mother asks behind him.

"Not yet," peeps Herman.

It just keeps on coming. It is impossible to stop. Now it runs over the top. The nurse comes running with a new glass, they change, and Herman is still not empty. Mother circles nervously around him. Herman stares at the wall. He has never peed for so long. Soon the next glass is full too. The doctor grabs two coffee cups. Herman fills them in a flash, and everyone runs back and forth shouting to each other. The doctor fetches the plant on the window sill. Herman waters it thoroughly, and finally it comes to an end. The last few drops run down over the leaves. The doctor wipes the sweat off his forehead and has to lie down awhile on the mattress.

"All done," Herman says, does up his fly and smiles happily at Mother. "Now it must be your turn."

By then the doctor is on his feet, coming toward him with a syringe in his hand. Herman gets goose bumps under his feet. He backs up and runs into the nurse, who puts her hands heavily on his shoulders.

"You lied," says Herman, pointing right at the doctor.

"This isn't a needle," he tries. "We're just going to take a blood sample."

"It looks the same."

"Maybe you'd like to sit down?"

"I'll stand where I am."

"Alright. Now we just tense our muscle so we can find a blood vessel."

But it's easier said than done. They must search high and low, and the doctor pinches and squeezes him all over. And suddenly he sticks the needle right through his skin and draws out the blood.

"I'm going to faint now," says Herman softly.

"You're doing just fine," whispers Mother, but she doesn't look particularly well either.

"Now I'm fainting," Herman says, collapsing straight to the floor.

When he comes to, he's lying on the mattress with a damp cloth on his forehead and a bottle of Coca-Cola within reach. At first he thinks it was all just a dream, that he came to, but to somewhere else, not to himself. He recognizes the doctor and nurse, but Mother looks different than before. Her face is as white as a tennis ball, and she has to support herself against the wall. But when he hears voices, he's quite certain that he's come to himself, just not at home. And the cola doesn't taste too bad.

"Have you noticed hair loss earlier?"

"Not that I know," Mother says quietly.

"You haven't found hair in the drain or on the comb?"

"Well, there's been a little, but I didn't think much about it."

"I can't say anything for certain until we've done some tests. But you ought to be prepared for the worst—that all the hair will fall out."

Everyone looks over at Herman. Mother comes closer and bends down.

"Are you awake, Herman?"

"I think so. We should drink the cola first."

Afterward, they are shown out, and everyone in the waiting room has gotten sicker. They almost aren't able to sit upright on the chairs, and they moan to each other and roll their eyes.

"It doesn't hurt much," Herman says. "Just a little."

Outside, it has just started to rain, an autumn rain that clings to the face like spider webs. Mother holds his hand so tight that it almost hurts, and her face is still far away, like a tennis ball hit over the rooftops. Herman tries to picture Mother without hair. It's impossible.

"You were very good," Mother clears her throat.

"You weren't so bad either."

Then he hears a strange sound and he must take a peek up. It's hard to see whether she's crying or if it's just the rain.

"Don't worry, Mother," says Herman. "You can buy a wig if too much falls out."

Now it's certain that she is crying, and on Bydgøy Avenue she stumbles on a chestnut and doesn't look to the right or the left.

"You can have red hair!" says Herman loudly. "Red hair is the best."

And he takes Mother safely across the street.

There is chicken for dinner and ice cream for dessert. But there is something Herman doesn't quite understand. Now Father's face is strange too, and sometimes he speaks English, and that never bodes well. Herman gets to stay up till nine-thirty, and Father tells him he's already bought first row tickets for *Zorro* and asks if he wants a sword and black mask. All things considered, they're so strange that Herman is almost relieved when he has to go to bed. They both come to his room, and Father does tricks with the chestnuts so fast that two get lost. And then Herman must console him too.

5.

FIVE ROPES HANG DOWN from the ceiling. Egg has a wide stance with his hands on his hips and the whistle in his mouth. Herman tries to sneak to a place in the very back, sinks his head down between his shoulders until only hair sticks up. But deep inside he knows it won't work, exactly the opposite. Every time he tries to become invisible it's somehow like everyone suddenly looks at him even more. Now Egg has fastened his eyes, curls his finger and spits out the whistle.

"Herman, are you playing hide-and-seek?"

"Not that I know."

"Come here, Herman."

"I'm fine here, thanks."

Egg smiles broadly and that's never good.

"I mean *here*, Herman."

"Yes, sir."

The gym shoes itch when he walks the eight steps over to Egg. He stops there. Egg was once a gymnast. Now the muscles hang in bags on his body. It's said that the last thing he did as a gymnast was an unfortunate jump over the vaulting horse. He always speaks in falsetto.

"Now you're going to climb up the rope until you hit the ceiling with that little head of yours.

Herman whispers:

"But that can't be done."

Egg bends down and bares all his teeth.

"I didn't hear what you said, Herman."

"Can't be done."

"Can't be done? Is that what you said? Why can't it be done, Herman?"

He shows his arm with the plastic bandage where the doctor drew blood.

"It doesn't work anymore," Herman says.

Egg lifts Herman's arm, looks at it closely, and suddenly, while the smile covers his entire face like a snake that has just swallowed an ox, he rips off the bandage. Herman screams inside and clenches his teeth until his molars crackle.

"Are you a sissy, Herman?"

Herman doesn't answer. He can hear someone just barely beginning to laugh.

"Are you a sissy, Herman?"

Herman looks up at Egg, in one eye, and in the pupil he discovers the reflection of the entire gymnasium, everyone standing behind him, pressing closer, and he can see himself, with a huge head and little legs, like a fly, but he cannot see Egg.

"Would you rather have gym with the girls?"

Now the laughter is completely released. Egg waves the bandage. There is a little spot of blood on it. Herman turns around, goes to the middle rope, and the laughter dies. But the silence is even worse. It's full of broken glass and is somehow invisible. Herman takes hold of the rope with both hands, closes his eyes and lifts himself up. He presses his knees together, fastens a new grip, his breath already getting thin. His arms ache. His heart is a dynamo. A white, painful light shines behind his eyes. He must open them, and at that instant the gymnasium tumbles around. He loosens his fingers and he slides down or up while his hands burn. He lands on his back and Egg stands over him.

"You dare to shower with the rest, Herman? You're like a girl."

There's a line in front of the mirror in the locker room,

and Glenn stands in front. He folds his hair backwards, attempts to twist a lock down his forehead. He looks angry and suddenly turns. The others make room for him, and he goes over to Herman, who is sitting on the bench, struggling with the last button on his shirt.

"Let me borrow your comb," Glenn says.

Herman pulls on his sweater, and when he gets his head through, everyone is standing around him.

"Let me borrow your comb!"

"Comb?"

"The steel comb. Come on!"

"No," Herman says.

Glenn looks around and grins.

"I don't want to borrow it," he says. "I want to have it."

Herman puts on his raincoat, but as he is about to take his southwester down from the peg, Glenn nabs it.

"You don't need a comb," he says. "'Cause you almost don't have any hair."

Herman looks up. Glenn throws the southwester into the shower.

"I got a haircut the day before yesterday," Herman says quietly.

"Then he messed up. You've got a bald spot!"

Everyone comes closer. Glenn holds Herman's head and bends it forward.

"Herman's got a bald spot! Herman's bald!"

Everyone shouts at the same time. Herman shakes his head lose. Glenn sneers.

"I'm sure you can borrow Ruby's hair. Red hair!"

The bell rings and everyone storms up the stairs. Herman remains sitting. He hears the laughter slowly disappear, but an echo remains in his ears. He puts his hand up carefully and feels, digs with his fingers and touches something smooth and irregular. He pulls his arm back and hides it under his raincoat. Now it is quiet again and he begins to understand. He begins to understand the connection. He gets his southwester and sneaks over to the mirror, bends his head and turns his eyes up, but he can't see anything. He wants to lift his hand but doesn't dare. Instead he pulls the yellow southwester on hard and ties it as tight as he can under his chin. He looks quickly in the mirror. His eyes are dark. Then he discovers Egg, and Herman turns slowly.

"Hustle! The bell's rung!"

Herman slings his gym bag over his shoulder and walks toward the door.

"Didn't you hear what I said? The bell has rung!"

Herman pauses. He has never known the smell to be so strong before, the sweat smell, sour, sickly, and he thinks of all the other smells and senses them at once, like an incredibly disgusting stink: the glue in Shop, rotting leaves, Father's deodorant, burnt fish, Grandfather's bedpan, the blood at the doctor's office, and the hair tonic at the barber's.

He looks at Egg.

"Why do we call you Egg?" Herman asks.

Egg loses his face and must screw it in place.

"Egg?"

"Egg, Egg."

"Do you call me Egg?"

"Yes, Egg."

Herman goes up the stairs. The cleaning lady is there with her rear in the air, and he gets the urge to kick her. But before he gets there she has picked up the bucket and gone her way.

The schoolyard is deserted. He can see faces behind all the windows. It's raining. The rain is silent before it hits the southwester and drips slowly in front of his face. He tries to see himself in the drops, but sees nothing, just shiny, transparent tears that extend out and fall. The knot under his chin becomes wet and even tighter. A window is thrown open. Barrel stands there. Herman doesn't see him, walks past the drinking fountain and out to the curve at Holte Street where leaves stick to the streetcar tracks. And the streets are deserted too. Herman is the last human on Earth. When he gets to Bonde Hill, a black cat crosses the cobblestones right in front of him and is gone under a fence. Someone has lost an umbrella just as black; it rolls down the sidewalk with broken wings.

But then he hears odd steps and he is no longer alone. At the bottom of the hill is the Lady with the Fleas. She waddles in her way and is coming toward him. Herman quickstops, slips around the corner and hides. His heart is completely out of sync, and the knot is so tight he almost can't breath. He hears her coming, closer and closer, and suddenly she is standing there, at the corner, resting on her crutches, turning slowly toward Herman, as if she has known all along where he was. Her hat is wrapped in transparent plastic, and newspaper sticks up out of her shoes. Now she's opening her mouth, and it amazes Herman that she can speak.

"Why are you afraid of me?"

Herman takes off and storms past her, down to Gyldenløves Street, and there he runs under the trees to Frogner Park. A horse comes toward him, a horse without a rider. The ground quivers, and the huge animal shines in the rain and is gone between the tree trunks. Herman thinks that on such a day, everything disappears. It rains incessantly, rains incessantly, and soon it's his turn to disappear, like a cat, an old umbrella, a horse.

Then he's standing under the tree again, and all the leaves have fallen. The branches are thin, dark fingers that scrape the clouds. It looks like a scarecrow or a ghost in the middle of the night when all the radios are turned off and the last lamp dimmed. Herman looks around, no people, just statues that stare at him with swollen eyes. He sprints down to the bridge and leans over the parapet. The ducks are moving around, and all the swans have lost their necks and heads. Herman pulls up the steel comb.

"Indian giver," he says inside.

And then he throws it as far as he can. It curves in an arc through the rain and hits a duck in the top of the head. It gives a little shriek, capsizes and sinks with the comb. But a short while later it pops up again and staggers up on shore. Herman looks at the *Sinnataggen* next to him. The *Sinnataggen* doesn't blab. The *Sinnataggen* is a friend, an only friend. But then he hears a sound from the other side and spins around. It's Ruby. She has already seen him. It's too late to take off. She stops, shakes water out of her hair and is serious.

"Are you going somewhere?"

She points at the gym bag.

"Maybe," says Herman.

"Where?"

"Adapazari."

"What are you taking with you?"

Herman hesitates.

"Gym shoes, sweatshirt and shorts."

Ruby laughs and comes closer. Then she doesn't laugh anymore.

"You skipped."

Herman doesn't answer.

"Barrel was pretty mad."

"Are you following me?"

"Why should I follow you?"

Herman doesn't know.

"Come," says Ruby.

They walk down to the water. Ruby takes off her school bag and finds her lunch. Then she spies out over the lake and begins to chatter. Right away a duck hobbles over to her and eats bits of hot dog. It chews a long time, then wades out and floats sideways along the shore.

Ruby turns toward Herman.

"That's my duck. It broke its wing."

Herman doesn't quite understand why, but he's suddenly glad. He sits down on the wet ground, yanks the knot under his chin forward and puts it in his mouth. It tastes good. The duck is still now, at a list, as if it's leaking. Ruby eats the rest of the sandwich.

"Don't you like red hair?" she suddenly asks.

Herman coughs out the knot.

"Red hair?"

Ruby's eyes narrow.

"Is it true that you have a bald spot?"

Herman stares at her. The red hair begins to burn even though it's raining. It glows like a huge halo.

"No, and that's final!"

"Let me see!"

She is going to pull off his southwester. Herman holds it tight and kicks her away. Ruby rolls around and stands on her knees in the mud. She snarls and laughs at the same time.

"You are bald! You are bald!"

Then she gets up without a word, walks up the hill and disappears behind the statues. Herman sits in the same place. It rains. He sees the duck out there. It moves diagonally in smaller and smaller circles. He remains sitting that way until it is cold down his back and the darkness rises from the ground. Then he walks past the restaurant, where the chairs are cleared away for good, and out to Frogner Square. Soon all the lamps are lit and the wind sweeps the wet, yellow light along the sidewalk. He isn't set on going home; it is just one place to go.

He goes to Grandfather's.

The door is always open there. He pushes it open carefully and squeezes into the dark entry. He can already hear that Grandfather is sleeping; small bubbles break between his thin blue lips. Herman continues into the room and sits down by the canopy bed. There lies Grandfather. That's all he can do. He has almost the same color as milk diluted with water, and Herman imagines that there is more water every day that passes. Soon Grandfather will be invisible. Then he turns his face slowly toward Herman, opens his eyes and wants to smile.

"Is that you, Herman? Have I slept all day."

"It's me. It's Thursday."

"Is it raining much?"

"It isn't snowing yet, Grandfather."

They are both quiet awhile. Half a fish cake lies on the night table. Herman eats it. It's a little stiff at the edges.

"Are you gong to take off your southwester?" Grandfather asks.

"Think I'll keep it on."

"That's just as well. There might be a shower."

"Does it rain in the canopy bed too?"

"It can happen," says Grandfather. "But most often it's dry

in these parts."

He pulls out a Queen chocolate and hands it to Herman. They each suck a long time on a bit, and Grandfather gets a little color in his face.

"Your daughter's a liar."

Grandfather swallows and his Adam's apple sticks out like a shark fin.

"What did you say, Herman?"

"Your daugther's a liar. Dirty liar."

Are you talking about your Mother now, Herman?"

"She's not my Mother. She just found me in a bathtub in Oslo Fjord."

"Why are you so mad, Herman?"

"Can't say."

"Okay. You can tell me about it some other time. Some other time."

Grandfather starts to drift off to sleep, then comes up from the pillow again.

"Have I told you about that friend of mine who won the grand prize in the railroad lottery right before the war?"

"Yes."

"Indeed. Martin, that's his name, he was a decent fellow. No nonsense with him. The pay envelope always came home to his wife whole and intact. But this day he had to pick up the tab, you know, for us boys. And it went on and on, as it usually does. But finally he got away, and he wanted to tell his wife about the prize so bad that he took a short-cut, across Bislet Stadium, from the southern to northern turns. He lived at Kiellands Square, you see. But he never got there. He got a discus in the back of the head and died instantly."

"And his wife got the prize."

"A trip for two on the Bergen Railroad. What I was going to say is that your parents have been here, Herman. They're looking for you."

Then Grandfather closes his eyes, hides his mouth and folds his hands on the comforter. Herman looks at the bald head. It resembles a soccer ball that the air has begun to leak from. He must bend forward and feel it, can't leave it alone.

First a finger. Then he lays his whole hand on the head. It is a little damp, and he can feel something that beats weakly; the thin skin quivers. Then Grandfather opens one eye and smiles in the corner of his mouth on the other side of his face. Herman draws in his arm and lays it in his lap.

"Relax," whispers Grandfather. "It's solid stuff."

When Herman turns around the street corner, a police car waits outside the entrance to his house, and a bunch of people with long necks and loud voices have gathered there. He is about to stop and slink backwards up Gables Street, but a window opens with a bang, and today the Bottle Man is loud mouthed. He swings a beer bottle in front of his red face and shrieks:

"Here he is! Here's the Claw! The Claw lives!"

Mother dashes out of the crowd where arms go up in the air. She lands on her knees in front of Herman and clasps her hands around him.

"Where have you been, Herman!"

"A ways."

"We have been so worried about you!"

Now Father comes too, and after him all the neighbors and the rest of the street, and at last two policemen who clear their way and each slip a hand down on Herman's southwester.

The older of them, with a bigger moustache than Nansen, bends down and uncovers his mouth.

"So this is Herman. We've been looking for you."

"I wasn't playing hide-and-seek."

The second policeman looks at Mother, and now Father is also at eye level, and it's starting to get crowded.

"I haven't seen you all day," says Father with a scorched voice. "Where in all the world have you been?"

Herman doesn't answer. The policeman raises his moustache again.

"You didn't run into anyone? I mean, is there someone who, for example, offered you chocolate?"

"Yes," Herman says.

Both of the policemen crouch down and take off their caps.

"So you got some chocolate. Who gave it to you, Herman?"

Mother hugs Father and all the faces are half in the light from the street lamps.

"I'm not saying."

"Did you know him, the one who gave you the chocolate?"

"I know him very well."

"Were you at his house?"

"Yes."

"Have you been there before?"

"At times."

"Did you get more than chocolate, Herman?"

"Yes."

Now the street is silent. The police inch closer.

"Can you tell us what it was?"

Herman looks away.

"Fish cake."

"He's been to Grandfather's!" Mother shouts and pushes her face forward. "But we were there too! Where were you earlier?"

"I'm not saying."

The Bottle Man has almost fallen out of the window, and his hair is full of foam now.

"I think the *pojken* has been to a rendezvous! Doesn't he have lipstick on his cheek!"

Then Jacobsen Jr. stands up and clenches his fist.

"Shut up, you drunk! And don't speak Swedish on our street!"

The Bottle Man shakes the foam off.

"I speak only Norwegian with the King!"

It doesn't take long to get the Bottle Man indoors. Later the policemen drive away slowly, and Herman stands between the hands of Mother and Father. It has stopped raining.

"Let's go home now," says one of them.

The globe shines in the window. Herman lies in bed with

a cup of cocoa next to him. Mother twists the film around a spoon and gives it to Father, who sucks on it a long time. Aren't you going to take off the southwester?"

Herman lets the cocoa stand and doesn't answer.

"It looks a little strange with pajamas and the southwester."

"No one can see me," says Herman.

Father suddenly has his hands behind back and is very sneaky.

"Which one do you want?"

Herman is skeptical.

"Neither," he says.

There is a sword with a gilded handle, a cape, a wide brimmed hat and a black mask. Herman turns toward the wall.

"Zorro," Father mumbles.

Herman stares at the wall.

"I don't give a damn for Zorro."

He lies on his back and pulls the southwester down over his eyes. Mother pushes her lower lip forward and blows on her permanent.

"Are you cursing, Herman?"

"When it fits."

Father hangs the equipment over the chair and his hands shake. Mother drinks up the cocoa, and afterward the silence is a candle burning at both ends.

Finally Father clears his throat and blows out the flame before the whole room catches fire. But it's Mother who begins to speak.

Herman, can you hear under the southwester?"

He doesn't answer. He squeezes his eyes shut and pulls the comforter over his face.

"I think you misunderstood a little, Herman. We didn't try to trick you. Do you understand?"

Herman barely peeks out. He sees the cape, the sword, the hat and the mask. And he can hear his heart beating, and it's actually quite eerie, just like the clock at Grandfather's. Does time stand still between each second? Or is it just creeping?

Mother continues talking. But it's just as if she has taken her voice to the cleaners and gotten the wrong one back.

"We don't know anything for certain yet. That's why the doctor took all the tests."

She has to turn away for a moment, and her neck is full of goose bumps. Then she moves the chair even closer to the bed.

"It isn't anything serious, but you might lose a little of your hair, Herman."

She tries to laugh. But her laughter doesn't sound like it should either.

"Do you remember what you said to me? We can buy a wig! Which color do you want, Herman? Red, green, brown or black?"

Herman stares at the ceiling and Mother gives up. Her hands fall vertically down in her lap with a swoosh. And then it is silent again. There soon won't be any silence left in the world. It's burning up with white, soundless flames.

"Can you say something, Herman?"

Mother has almost risen from the chair.

"Are you mad at us?"

Then Father suddenly bends forward with something in his hands.

"I found the chestnuts anyway," he tries to smile. "Know where they were? In my wallet! Don't know how they managed that."

He lays them on the comforter. Herman lets them lie.

"What are you going to do with all the chestnuts, Herman?"

"Put them in snowballs when it's winter."

"That's sneaky. But who are you going to throw the snowballs at?"

"You."

6.

FINALLY THE LIGHT FALLS, or it rises, slowly but surely. Herman counts silently to thirty before it's so dark that he can only see a hand in front of him, and in the hand he holds a candy bar. Then it gets very restless in the rows behind him, and a voice shouts:

"Take off that hat! We can't see anything!"

Father bends to Herman's ear.

"I think you'll have to take off the southwester, Herman. Otherwise there'll be trouble."

He coaxes it carefully down from his head and puts it in his lap. But now it's Father's turn. A thin voice in the auditorium is on the verge of crying.

"I can't see anything 'cause this dumb man is so tall!"

A mother hushes so lowly that everyone can hear it, and Herman's father sinks down in his seat, but then he doesn't have room for his knees and there is a commotion.

Then it flashes powerfully from a clear sky. The lightning forms big letters, all the chocolate bars are unwrapped at the same time, and a hissing sound twists like a snake along the rows: sh-sh-sh-sh-sh-sh-sh! And there rides Zorro. Everyone stomps in rhythm, and he rides right past them, lifting his sword in greeting, and disappears behind the screen while the moon rises over a dreary landscape where an invisible orchestra plays for dear life.

First Bernardo does some magic. He puts an egg in one ear of a donkey and pulls a coin out of the other. The egg is later discovered in the trousers of a man who at first sight looks like a bandit, and then the egg is broken. Father smiles crookedly and nudges Herman. Later Bernardo goes home to Zorro, who is really and truly a poet named Don Diego, and is able to relate that a beautiful lady is held captive in Monastario's castle. Zorro can't live with that for long. When dark falls and the inland city's only church bell rings twelve times, Bernardo helps him to change. Zorro fastens the cape on his back, whips the wide hat into place, sticks the sword in his belt, pulls the mask down over his eyes, and at last puts on the huge gloves that resemble the ones the traffic cops at Solli Square use.

Zorro is ready.

He hops right out the window and lands on Tornado, who fortunately is standing there. And then he rides off through the night, and the invisible orchestra continues playing while black clouds race back and forth across the sky where the moon hangs white and still.

The castle is on the top of a mountain. Zorro parks Tornado by a tree and sneaks the last bit on his own legs. At last he has to climb three hundred feet straight up. There he finds an opening he can barely eel his way through.

Zorro is inside the castle.

He stands in a corridor full of shadows and armaments. Somewhere not far away he can hear many loud voices and much laughter. But far below he hears something completely different: A woman crying, and judging by the fragile sound, it is a very pretty lady who is imprisoned here, exactly as Bernardo said.

Zorro finds a narrow, steep stairway, and he goes down it. A torch glows in a niche in the stone wall. He takes it with him. He can hear the crying more clearly now. He approaches the cell where the lady is held in captivity.

Zorro suddenly stops.

Footsteps. Heavy footsteps.

A figure comes into sight around the corner, a giant hunchback, one eye and two sharp-edged knives. The guard. They stand face-to-face, but not for long. Zorro throws the torch at him. The giant screams and falls backward, hits his head on the stone floor and remains there the rest of his time. But as Zorro is about to take the huge ring of keys from him, the enemy comes running from all sides and blocks all exits. Zorro draws his sword swiftly, and there is a hard battle with great loss of life. One by one they must give up, but more show up constantly, and Zorro is alone against the lot. At last he must give up. He is forced up against the wall by thirty-two furious men, and then Monastario himself comes into view. And it's the bandit Bernardo smashed the egg in the trousers of. He still has a big spot there.

Zorro is thrown into a cell without hesitation. The heavy door is pushed shut and six locks are twisted round before the footsteps and voices disappear in the castle above. Zorro can hear the lady moaning in the next cell. But then he hears another sound too, a machine that is started, rusty gears gripping each other. And then he sees with his own eyes: one of the stone walls begins to move. It comes toward him. The room gets smaller and smaller. It comes toward him, slowly. He attempts to hold it back, but it is useless. It just continues, closer and closer to Zorro, who now presses against the other wall, which doesn't stand still either.

Suddenly the entire screen is black. The silence in the theater can be felt, like a black, treacherous cat. It begins to crackle behind the screen, and then, in small writing down in the corner: *Continued next month.* A gigantic whistle concert breaks out, and chocolate wrappers, chestnuts and pocket lint pour down on the screen while the lights rise, or fall, from the lamps along the walls.

Herman whips on the southwester.

When they get outside, the sky is high and black and has a lot of stars, like a black man with freckles. A new line stands at the entrance, and Herman wants to tell them how it ended. But then he recognizes two figures on the sidewalk across the street. It's the doctor and the nurse. They're discovered under a lamp post, holding each other tightly, thinking maybe that no one can see them. Herman thinks. It isn't so strange that they both have a cold at the same time. The Disen street-car stops, and when it drives away the doctor is alone. He doesn't see Herman. His eyes are somewhere other than his head.

"I think Zorro will manage," Father says. "But it sure isn't fun to stand there a whole month."

They turn down Gabels Street and get a salt wind in their faces.

"I suppose you'll try out the equipment now, hmm?"

Herman doesn't answer, but Father continues to talk up there. Maybe one chats with oneself a great deal when one is a crane operator.

"There'll certainly be a lot of apples this year. We'll have to take at least a bag each. Big bags. Maybe we'll have to make two trips to the dock. But we'll take a taxi from City Hall, right? Hope it's a Mercedes. Mind if I smoke, Herman?"

Father stops and searches all his pockets. But when he goes to light the match, it blows out every time. At last Herman has to come and shield the match with his hands. He stands on his toes while Father bends his knees, and the flame lights up their faces. Herman doesn't know why, but he suddenly wants to cry. He puts the knot in his mouth instead, and Father puffs out a cloud of smoke.

"Do you think Mother's made something good for when we get home?" he asks.

"Burnt jello," says Herman.

And Father doesn't want to say any more.

7.

HERMAN SITS UNDER an apple tree. The ground is wet, but the sky is dry; the sun sees to that. It hangs like a white shield over Oslo Fjord. Herman would prefer rain, hard rain. Now the air is so clear that he can count every stone at Kols Ridge. He doesn't bother to. Instead, he follows a plane with his eyes. It takes off from Fornebo, and is no bigger than a slender hummingbird when it disappears toward America. I should have been on it, Herman thinks in his quiet mind. And nothing is as quiet as the mind.

Then he suddenly gets hit in the middle of the skull. It doesn't hurt particularly since he has the southwester on. It isn't a glass apple, since it doesn't break. Instead it just rolls out on the grass and lies there without a sound, so it's not a grenade either. Herman looks up. Father is balancing on the top branch, shaking down apples.

"You coming up?" he calls.

But Herman remains sitting. He can't get Zorro out of his head. What would Herman do if he were in the same boat? He has no idea. But Zorro will surely find a way. Maybe Bernardo can get him out with magic? Herman picks up the apple. It's green and smooth. The moon must be this smooth. He is about to take a bite, but stops before he gets his mouth open. How can one know whether there is a worm in an apple or not before he has taken a bite? Then maybe one won't find a worm, but half a worm. He goes down to Mother instead, who waves to him from the well.

When he gets there, she points in the grass with the rake. "Look there," she says.

Herman looks. There's a porcupine under some brown leaves. The head isn't visible, but it has all its quills out. It looks like a pin cushion that the world's biggest seamstress must have lost along the way. He touches it carefully with his finger tips. Nothing happens.

"Dead and gone," says Herman.

"Oh, no it's not. The porcupine's just sleeping. It's settled here for the winter."

Then they hear a noise, and a tall man flutters through the air. He lands on his back and remains there. Herman and Mother run up to the tree, but before they get there, Father is already on his feet, shaking off apples, grass and twigs.

"Are you hurt?" Mother wants to know immediately.

"No, Mom. People have fallen from higher. So let's get the rucksacks!"

Later, Herman stands in the big summer cabin where it smells of old magazines, seaweed and apples. The light falls in through the four windows, long columns, diagonally down to the floor. It resembles something he has seen: the drawing in *The Illustrated Bible* at school. The sun always shines that way whenever Jesus is there. A few insects wake up, butt against the windowpanes and fall down to the sill again. Then Herman hears rummaging outside. A ladder stands up outside the first window, and Father comes into view with one of the shutters, which he screws into place. And that's the way Herman remembers this Sunday, which wasn't altogether memorable, but he doesn't forget it anyway. He has this feeling deep inside—so deep that he has barely been there before—that something is gone, that something is ended, or is beginning. Herman stands in the middle of the floor, with the yellow southwester on his head, while Father closes the windows, one by one, and the darkness grows around him like a thick forest. Finally only the door out to the porch is open, and his parents pop up there like two shadows, or silhouettes against the sharp autumn sun far away. They hug each other, and look into the darkness, but Herman doesn't know if they can see him.

"That's it," says Father.

He says it just like that: That's it. And Herman knows that he won't forget those words either. That's it.

WINTER

8.

HERMAN IS AWAKENED by the snow, and he is wide awake immediately. He stays in bed, listening. He can hear the snow falling over the city like a weak breath. Otherwise everything is silent. It is almost night still. The streetcars haven't begun running, and his parents are sleeping. He tries to remember some of what he has dreamed, but can't do it now either.

He slips over to the window and peeks out. He wasn't wrong. It's snowing. The streets are already white, and there isn't a footprint or wheel track anywhere to be seen. Herman follows a snowflake with his eyes, but gets dizzy. It's almost like being on a carousel with one's head in a flour sack. He staggers back to the bed, and then he discovers it: something lying on the pillow. He looks closer. It's hair, a whole clump of hair. His hands rush up to his head. He has to sit down. He looks at his fingers. Hair. There is hair everywhere. The entire room is full of hair. He can't catch his breath. He heads for the bathroom, but all he can see in the mirror is the northern hemisphere, and that's not enough. He fetches two kitchen chairs and balances them on top of each other. Then he climbs up on the edge of the bathtub, steadies himself against the medicine cabinet and places himself on the top chair. Now he can see it clearly. The hair has fallen from his own head. Right under the part is a bare spot. It shines like a polished crown. Herman bends even closer to the mirror to be certain that it really is him. It is, because when he closes his eyes, the face in the mirror does exactly the same.

Then the chairs tumble. Herman hears everything at once: his own terrified yell, his parents suddenly awakening, the mirror being broken and the snow continuing to fall.

Someone shakes him, harder and harder. Herman opens his eyes. He's sitting on the toilet. It's Mother on her knees in front of him, and her nightgown is red with yellow dots. She looks like a huge ladybug. Herman begins counting the dots, for then he can find out how old he is.

"Herman, Herman, are you hurt?"

"One landed safely."

Now Father is there too. His pajamas are yellow with red dots. He looks like a serious outbreak of the measles. He sweeps up the shards of glass on a tray.

"It means bad luck for forty days and forty nights," Herman says.

"What in the world were you trying to do here?" Mother asks.

"Someone scalped me during the night," Herman says softly.

Now Mother sees it too, the bare spots above the ear, as big as a drain plug. She raises her hand and is about to feel his head, but then it's as if she doesn't dare. She hides her hands in each other and her face goes through many changes. Father has also become curious. He comes closer, and Herman gets dizzy from all the dots around him.

"It's almost unnoticeable," whispers Mother. "If you comb your hair like this."

"Let me go!"

"But Herman . . ."

"Let go! Let go!"

He pushes her away and runs back to his room. The clump of hair lies on the pillow. It looks like a dead and rotting mouse. He tries to squeeze it back in place, but it's no good. The hair drifts down on the floor, and outside the window it's snowing even heavier. Herman gathers the hair up and puts it in the bottom drawer where he also has all the chestnuts.

And now the rest of the world wakes up: The Bottle Man opens the day's first beer. Barrel puts chalk and five sandwiches in his briefcase. Woody seals a love letter to the cleaning lady and Egg does three-and-a-half push-ups. The Lady with the Fleas is already out walking since she takes twice as long no matter where she's going. Jacobsen Jr. puts the ballpoint pens in place in his coat. Fats pulls two hairs out of his left nostril. Ruby carefully takes off her hair net, and Grandfather eats the rest of a Queen chocolate and falls back to sleep.

Herman lays down too. He is never going to get up again. That's what he has decided. He is a porcupine almost without quills.

A half hour later Mother stands there.

"Herman, don't you want to go to school today?"

He doesn't answer.

"You can stay home if you like, but then I'd better call and tell them. Since we're going to the doctor again tomorrow, you know."

"We don't have a telephone."

"I can call from the store."

Herman thinks about it. He thinks about it hard.

"I'm not a sissy," he says at last.

Father still hasn't gone to work. He's drinking coffee and has cut his finger. It's wrapped in a bandage, so he has to hold the cup with his left hand and spills every time he lifts it.

Mother has boiled eggs, and she usually only does that on Sundays. But Herman understands the connection. Next to the plate is a big bottle of cod-liver oil. He closes his eyes and may as well take a swallow. It tastes like gym shoes and old bologna. He sends the bottle on to Father, who looks at Mother surprised, but he can't get out of it. He grimaces over his entire face and has to drink three cups of coffee afterward and spills even more.

Herman is going to decapitate the egg, but stops before the knife hits the shell. It's just like with the apple. How can one know whether there is a chicken in there or not? By the time he has divided it in two, it's too late. And then he starts thinking about the gym teacher and doesn't want the egg at all. He pushes it as far away as possible. Then Father's eyes get wily. He takes the egg, closes his hand around it, makes many movements with both arms, both in front and behind him, and stands up in the meantime. Then he displays his hands, and there is absolutely nothing in them. They are empty as piggy banks. They have to give him applause.

"Call me Bernardo," Father says proudly.

But when he sits down they hear something crush nastily, and the light in his face changes very quickly to red. Eyes roam in all directions, and he stands up with a bowed head.

"It's no good conjuring with a bandage on the finger," he mumbles, and shuffles stoop-shouldered to the bathroom.

On the chair is a fresh omelet. Herman begins to laugh. He doesn't know where the laughter comes from. It just grows inside him, like a balloon, and he has to get the laughter out. Soon he's screaming of laughter, and now Mother is laughing too. They laugh until they're almost on all fours under the table. But then Father is at the door again, and he isn't laughing, since he only has undershorts on and looks unhappy. And then Mother has to help him find new trousers. She goes with him, hiccuping. Herman suddenly feels that the laughter is caught in his throat, like a crossways fish bone, or maybe he has his heart in his throat instead, and that's even worse. But in any case it's fortunate there was no chicken in the egg.

Mother comes back with her hands behind her back.

"You can't wear the southwester any longer, Herman."

"Want to bet?"

"It's snowing. I've set out your boots. And look what's finished!"

She tosses the cap over to him. It is blue, with a huge tassel in three colors. It is the biggest tassel Herman has seen. It's bigger than a piassava broom. It's even bigger than Ruby's hairdo.

"Aren't you going to try it on?" Mother asks.

He looks around quickly. Then he loosens the knot under his chin, flings off the southwester and pulls the cap on lightning fast.

"Does it fit?"

"Pretty good," says Herman, and the tassel is so heavy that he almost loses his balance.

Father sticks in his face, and he has gotten his smile back again.

"Shall we walk together, Herman? Wow! What a nice cap! Take many years to make that, Mom?"

She boxes him in the stomach, but it doesn't look like it hurts much, about like crashing with a butterfly.

"Be careful today," she says softly.

They walk slowly through the snow. The snow boots make tracks with crooked stripes. At the Bottle Man's, the shades are still down. He can't stand snow. He usually goes out only once a winter, and that's when the Christmas beer comes to Jacobsen's Grocery.

Father is on a soapbox even though he's walking down the middle of the sidewalk.

"Mother's always afraid when it snows. That I'll slip and fall. But no danger there. It's like a ladder on all the sides, you know. Four ladders that are welded together in a square. You sort of climb inside the ladder. Pretty smart. Soon it'll be your turn, Herman. Come on down one day after school when the weather's good. I've talked to the foreman. Not that I needed to talk to him first, it just happened that way, you know. How about sometime next week?"

Herman shrugs his shoulders and gets a cramp in the stomach. It growls over the luminous belt buckle, but Father hears nothing.

"I really should have been a pilot, you now that? A pilot. Do you know what a pilot and I have in common?"

Herman chooses to answer no.

"Depth perception."

"Depth perception?"

"Exactly. Depth perception. Not everyone has it, you understand. When I'm up in the crane's cabin, looking straight down, I have to be able to see whether one pillar is three centimeters higher than the others. Otherwise it's screwed up. Then it's crash, boom, bang.

They stop on the corner where they each go their own way. Herman stares down at his boots, but one must have to be a lot higher up to tell if he has depth perception.

Father spics around.

"Poor visibility," he concludes. "Probably be mostly the barracks today."

They don't say any more for awhile, kick at the snow, and somehow can't get loose. Jacobsen Jr. parks his Triumph outside the grocery store, polishes the hood a little, tips his hat and lets himself in.

"Show-off," Father says between his teeth. "Milksop. Pomade in his hair too."

He suddenly shuts up and carefully squints down at Herman. The lights come on in the store and they can hear American music from the back room. Father takes a peek at the clock and clears his throat loud and long.

"Think there'll be a world's record in the ten thousand this year?"

Herman doesn't answer.

"Kuppern can do it, if you ask me."

Herman doesn't ask him.

Father kicks more snow.

"How's it going, Herman?"

"Nothing special."

Then they go their own ways, but turn and watch each other awhile like they usually do. It's snowing so hard that they can barely see each other. They wave anyway.

Herman waits on Harelabben until the bell rings. He starts to regret coming and wants most of all to turn and go home again. But then a voice calls from a window, and that voice belongs to the principal, and the principal is not to be fooled with. He was a second lieutenant in the military and won many big battles.

"Hey you. Yes, you there! With the cap! Get to class this minute!"

A telephone rings behind him, and he remains standing in the window with the receiver in his hand while Herman takes off and stampedes inside.

And as usual, he's the last. But he has heard somewhere, perhaps it was the radio one Sunday morning or on the Request Concert, that the last shall be the first. It didn't register until now. He hangs his jacket on the peg and opens the door carefully without knocking. Barrel has already rolled down the map of Norway. His back is to the door, so Herman sneaks past the teacher's desk toward the window row. But each time he takes a step, a new sucking sound comes from his boots. It sounds like an elephant eating jello. Barrel does an about-face that takes at least a couple of minutes, and opens his eyes wide.

"Halt!" he commands.

But Herman has already sat down and is looking out the window. White is a remarkable color, for really it's no color at all. But he can see the snow anyway. It hangs motionless in the air, little, thin flakes. Maybe God has sunned himself too much above the clouds where the sky is blue, and his shoulders are peeling.

Barrel is out on the floor, clapping the chalk off his hands.

"Are we seeing this. Herman's come. And what delayed you today? Not another fox, I hope?"

The laughter begins with Glenn and spreads like a knife in warm butter. It's Ruby who finally laughs the loudest.

Barrel stops the laughter with a raised hand.

"Or maybe you ran into a quarrelsome polar bear on Bygdøy Avenue?"

Herman finds no reason to answer. Barrel grips the pointer and pumps himself up.

"Are you cold?"

"No, thanks."

"Are you *cold,* I asked!"

"No, thank you very much."

"Can you be so very kind as to take off your cap!"

Herman looks out the window again. Maybe soon he'll be hanging out there by the left ear for forty minutes.

"I didn't hear what you said?" Barrel shouts.

"I didn't say anything either."

Barrel is just three feet away. He is twice as big as usual, and his eyes bulge out. That's something Herman has wondered about, whether Barrel can see his own feet when he's standing up. He can't have much depth perception in any case.

"*Take off your cap, Herman Fulkt!*"

"No, and that's final."

Barrel doesn't believe his own ears. For a moment he looks around in confusion. All the blood runs down from his head leaving behind a very pale face above. It's so quiet in the classroom that one could hear a porcupine breathing at Nesodden. Even Ruby has turned around, and her jaw hangs at half-mast.

"Did you say no?" whispers Barrel, bending down.

"Yes."

"Are you refusing?"

Suddenly Herman doesn't know how things got this way, when it began or what has led to Barrel's big mug coming closer and closer, with quivering lips, yellow teeth and sweat drops on the forehead. Who is to blame? He only knows that he is very frightened and that he never should have gone to school today.

"Are you refusing?" Barrel repeats, and soon he can't get any closer.

"If you hold me out the window, my ear will rip off," Herman whispers.

Barrel closes one eye tight and drops the pointer. Then he grabs the tassel and pulls, and Herman holds it down with both hands and shakes his head for all he's worth.

Then the door suddenly opens and the principal marches in. Barrel lets go and has a fist full of three colors of yarn. Everyone stands at attention at their desks, except Herman. He remains sitting. Barrel clears his way to the front, stands next to the principal and hides his hand behind his back.

The principal looks around quickly, holds his eyes on Herman awhile, then moves his eyes straight forward again.

"I have come to talk about snowballs! There is wet snow now, and I have the following to say: One thrown snowball gives two days detention. Two thrown snowballs gives detention for as many days *and* repetition for one day. Three thrown snowballs will result in a letter home, eventually suspension for four days, depending on the snowball's target. Understand!"

No one answers. It means that everyone has understood. Barrel wipes the sweat off his forehead and takes the floor from the principal.

"As you see, there is a pupil in this class who is being impossible today. He absolutely. . ."

The principal takes the floor back, pulls Barrel with him out in the hall and closes the door.

It isn't long before Barrel comes in again, alone, and he is somehow punctured. He slinks up to the teacher's desk and sits heavily. He glances carefully over to Herman and wants to be friendly. Then Herman becomes even more frightened. He wants to sink into the ground then and there, or crawl down in the ink well and screw the lid defensively after himself.

Barrel isn't even able to get the pointer. He lifts the biggest of his fingers to the map and speaks slowly.

So, this is Norway, which has many great men. And as you can see, Norway is a far flung country. It is as far from Oslo to Hammerfest in the north as it is from here to eternity, I mean Rome. And here, on the Oslo Fjord, is the little city that Herman comes from. I mean Herman Wildenvey, the poet from Stavern. 'And there is little Selma. She is truly worth a song.' "

The bell rings before he gets much further and everyone storms the door. Herman is the last again. He takes his school bag under his arm and hurries past Barrel, who still studies the map of Norway.

"Wait a minute, Herman," he says.

But Herman has absolutely no desire to wait now that Barrel has gone crazy. He runs out to the hall, takes his jacket and spurts down the stairs, while Barrel calls after him.

Everyone in the schoolyard turns at the same time. Herman stops suddenly, and the heavy door slams shut with a bang behind him. But his heart beats even harder. His heart is a door that slams inside his jacket. He has to hold tight. It has stopped snowing. He can see Ruby over in the girl's shed. She has her hair hidden in her parka hood, and her eyes are popping out of her head. Glenn sits on the drinking fountain. On each side stand Karsten and Bjørnar.

Herman takes a step backwards, but inside is Barrel. He can't flee there either. He closes his eyes and walks out in the schoolyard. He counts to eight. He gets to fifteen. He starts to lose his bearings. He says twenty inside, and then the first snowball hits him in the middle of the neck. The cap gets pushed forward. He pulls it in place and opens his eyes. They have already encircled him. Glenn stands in front.

"Take off the cap, you sissy!" he says.

Herman doesn't do it. He tries to close his eyes again, but it doesn't help. He can see everything anyway because he already has seen it. The ring around him becomes tighter and tighter.

Glenn takes a step forward and boxes at the tassel. Karsten and Bjørnar come from behind. Herman tears himself free and holds the cap tight with both hands. Glenn tugs the tassel, and Herman is suddenly lying on the ground. He sees only feet stamping in rhythm, coming closer. Zorro is the only thing Herman has time to think of. Just like Zorro at Frogner.

"Let go of the cap!" Glenn yells.

But Herman doesn't let go. They'll have to kill him before he'll let go of the cap. He tries to kick, but it's no use. He is locked tight. He soon won't be able to breath. And far away, even though they're right next to him, he hears everyone shouting:

"Baldy! Baldy! Baldy!"

Glenn has gotten a better grip. The cap glides over his ears. Herman tears it the other way. But then something happens. The feet run in all directions. Two hands come into view, and Glenn is lifted up by both of the cauliflowers. It is Barrel's specialty. He carries Glenn, who screams and kicks in the air, over to the principal's office. And at the same time the bell rings. Herman is suddenly lying all alone, on his back, in the middle of the schoolyard. For a short while the clouds glide to the side, and he can see the sky is almost blue, like an old air mattress that's going flat.

Herman gets up slowly, shakes the snow off his clothes. He looks like a tired dog who has just come out of the water. The world is silent again. He straightens his cap, then goes down to the gym. There sits Egg in the locker room, polishing his whistle. Herman pauses in the door opening. Egg looks at him surprised, and it takes a little time for him to know who he has to deal with.

"Wrong time," says Egg. "Go away."

He continues to polish the little instrument.

"Getting my gym shoes, Egg," Herman says.

He finds them on the shelf over the sink, puts them in his school bag and is on the way out.

Egg stops him with a spongy hand. Egg is soft to run into. He almost has breasts. Once they must have been hard muscles.

"Why do you kids call me Egg?"

"Don't know, Egg."

"Does everyone call me Egg?"

"Yes, Egg."

Herman ducks under Egg's arm and takes off before any more is said. Afterward he goes down to the shop. He hears sounds in there that he is suspicious of. He has heard his parents do something like that some Saturdays. Herman pushes the door open. Woody sits on the table with the cleaning lady in both arms. He lets her go immediately, and she stumbles to the floor with a sigh of surprise.

Woody stares at Herman, who stands next to the wall looking sidelong under the edge of his cap.

"I . . . I was just showing her. . . the glue," says Woody, twisting his coat into place.

A burst of laughter comes from the cleaning lady, who stands up with broom and pail and hurries past Herman.

"Thanks for coming before I got stuck completely, little

guy!"

She runs up the stairs, and Woody's ears burn like two torches, one on each side of his head.

"What do you want!" he snarls.

"To get something."

Herman goes over to the cabinet and finds his herbarium in the bottom of the pile. He sticks it in his school bag and slings it on his back.

"You can't take it home now!"

"Yes one can," says Herman.

"But you haven't finished it!"

"It'll never be finished."

Woody gets a crossways wrinkle in his forehead.

"Why not?"

"Because I'm going to die in the meantime."

Woody drops his jaw, dumfounded, but not for long. His eyes become dark as the Black Sea. He barely keeps from swallowing his mouth.

"You're not fooling me again!"

"I'm fooling no one," Herman enlightens.

"And what's wrong with you today, hmm? A knife in the back maybe? And take off that cap when you're speaking to me!"

Woody comes toward him, but Herman is quicker. He slips away, tips over a pail of glue on the way, and Woody stands there pulling his shoes up from the floor as if he stepped in a huge wad of chewing gum.

"Punk!" he yells. "Punk! Just wait!"

Herman waits a moment, then strolls out calmly without turning.

Up in the corridor he hears voices. He stops, listens and peeks around the corner. There stands Barrel and the principal talking to the cleaning lady. She mentions his name several times, but points in the other direction. Barrel and the principal run that way. When they are out of sight, the cleaning lady turns and waves to Herman with her cloth, and he regrets that he once planned to kick her in the rump.

Herman walks toward home, and he takes many detours

so that no one will find him. He sneaks in a gate and through yards, and a nasty suspicion bothers him more and more. What was it the principal said to Barrel in the hallway? Why did Barrel quit chewing him out? Why didn't he hold Herman right out the window by the ear instead? On Oscars Street he walks backwards for safety's sake; if anyone tries to follow his footprints, they'll think he has turned. But he discovers other footprints in the snow there and has to stop to examine them more closely. There are two feet at least a yard apart and they point almost right in at each other. And on each side of the tracks is the mark of a cane. It is almost impossible to see which way they are going. Herman studies the tracks a long time, then he follows them down to Frogner Road, where they turn to the left and continue along the streetcar tracks all the way up to Langbreckes Street. The footprints stop there outside a shop. Herman looks up: *Frogner Pedicure and Beauty Salon.* He presses his face to the glass and shades his eyes with his hands. Inside is the Lady with the Fleas. She has her feet on a stool, and another lady is on her knees picking at her toes. A third lady pulls at her fingers. Herman holds his breath. Maybe they're looking for fleas? But he can't see any. There's a wash basin on the floor. That must be where they're putting the fleas when they get a hold of them.

Suddenly she turns, the Lady with the Fleas, and looks at the window. Herman ducks, but it's too late. She has already seen him. She doesn't look particularly angry, or very sad either, and that's almost worse. Herman takes a hold of his cap and sprints as fast as he can all the way to Drammen Road.

He reduces speed there, walks calmly past Jacobsen's Groceries without so much as looking inside. He still has this suspicion; who was it who called the principal this morning? Mother comes out and runs after him. Herman just continues walking. She catches up with him at the next corner, out of breath and flustered.

"Hi, Herman. Has something happened?"

"Not that I know."

He looks away. Mother comes around on the other side and isn't quite herself. He starts to understand now. No one shall believe they can fool Herman Fulkt so easily.

"The streetcar ran into Jacobsen Jr's car today. Dcntcd up the whole side. Junior didn't see the tracks because of the snow."

Herman listens with an ear and a half.

"There was almost a fist fight. He hit the conductor in the head with a carrot!"

Mother laughs loudly. Herman has decided not to laugh.

"Hey, what did you do to the tassel?"

"Nothing."

"But it's all gone!"

"You didn't sew it on very well. It fell off by itself."

Herman continues on while Mother remains standing at the same spot, watching him, but he doesn't turn around once. It starts to snow again, and Mother freezes as Herman slowly rounds the corner.

9.

HERMAN LIES ON HIS BACK and stares up at the ceiling. Only his eyes are visible between the comforter and the cap, two narrow dark stripes.

"You have to eat something," Mother says quietly.

Father holds out a slice of bread with both goat cheese and strawberry jam. It's no use. Herman clenches his fist under the comforter. Father walks out to the bathroom, washes his hands, changes shirts and comes back and eats the slice of bread himself. Mother smooths out the comforter. Outside it's already dark.

"I only wanted to help," she whispers.

"You told," Herman says. "You told the principal and now everyone knows!"

"I didn't mean to."

Mother's face is white as a bed sheet and her mouth is a dark spot.

"Were they mean to you, Herman?"

Herman continues to stare up at the ceiling, and it's just as if it's coming closer and closer, and he must reach out his arm to hold it away.

"No," he says.

Father has something on his heart, and it must be heavy. He's getting smaller and smaller where he sits. Soon his upper body will be between his knees. Mother nudges him with her elbow, and he starts talking as if he learned to yesterday.

"Herman. That comb, you know, the steel comb. Maybe it's not too smart, I mean, to use it now."

He gets stuck and Mother takes over.

"It's much too sharp and hard, you see. It probably isn't good for you. The doctor will surely say the same thing tomorrow."

Herman looks at them with one eye.

"You can have it back afterward, of course," says Father quickly. "When you. . .when you are. . .well."

Herman looks at them with both eyes.

"I threw it away," he says.

They bend closer with bewildered faces.

"What did you say, Herman?"

"Indian giver."

His parents sit awhile with dropped chins. Then they get up at the same time and go out quietly. Mother leaves the door ajar; a white stripe of light divides the room in two and thick shadows loom on each side.

"Close the door!" Herman shouts.

It is slowly pushed closed, and the stripe along the floor disappears with a sigh. Now only the globe on the windowsill is lit. Herman lies with open eyes, thinking that he will never sleep again. He'll be awake the rest of his life, until all his hair has fallen out and his skull is smooth as a globe, like a chestnut, like a moon. Then he'll be sent around in a traveling circus and shown in a cage along with the world's biggest dwarf and the zebra without stripes, and everyone who sees him will die of laughter.

The ceiling is back in place above him, but now it's Herman that is falling. Everything becomes darker and darker, as if he's sinking in a pool full of jellyfish. His eyelids are heavy as roof slates. He needs at least four crutches to hold them up. And soon all the sounds disappear—the streetcar on Drammen Road, the music from the radio, the voices in the apartments, the wind beneath the sky.

Then Herman decides to get up. Suddenly he's sitting on the windowsill, opening the window and climbing along the rain gutter. The streets are silent as old dreams. And when he walks in the snow, he leaves no footprints behind.

He doesn't need to take more than three steps, then he's at the construction site at Vika. The crane towers over him like a gaunt dinosaur standing on its hind legs eating the stars. He starts to climb inside the ladders. It's easy as nothing. He doesn't get dizzy at all. It's almost like he was weightless, like a bird, like a leaf. He gets the desire to let go and fly out into the dark, that's how it feels. It's so good that he must sing a verse from the Request Concert, but strangely enough, doesn't hear his own voice.

He crawls into the cab and looks out the window. Far below lies the city, with scattered lights that move all the time. He stretches his neck, but doesn't see either angels or America.

Then Herman sits down at the control levers, and he doesn't sing now. He hums silently instead and clenches his teeth. He guides the big arm around and lowers the hook. He thinks that he may as well begin with his parents. He lowers the hook over Svolder Street and lifts their bed out the window, almost loses them in the water at Dyna lighthouse, but finally places the bed in the biggest of the apple trees at Nesodden. They can just as well wake up there the next day and get up on the wrong side of the bed. Then he takes the doctor, and the doctor is not alone. The nurse is visiting. She snores in his arms. Herman fastens the hook around their arms, lifts them carefully and doesn't let them go until they are at Kikut. There they can lie in the snow and make their colds even worse. Now it's Barrel's turn. He lives on the fifth floor at Homansbyen, and Herman hangs him out the window by his ear. He flails his fat legs, howls and carries on, but doesn't get out a single sound. Herman lets him hang there and taste his own medicine. Then he gets Glenn, Karsten and Bjørnar, hoists them up and down before he decides to drop all three in the school toilets. Egg and Woody are quickly disposed of, getting to spend the night in the glue bucket so they have to go around the rest of their lives like Siamese twins. Herman doesn't really know what to do with Fats, but for safety's sake he swings the barber up to Holmenkollen and puts him at the top of the ski jump. But Herman has plans for Ruby. He lifts her by her hair and places her on the top of the Monolith. Then five red birds fly out of her hairdo and it sinks together like a punctured balloon on her head.

But he lets Grandfather, the Bottle Man and the Lady with the Fleas rest in peace tonight. Some other time he'll lift them too. Grandfather will even get to choose where his canopy bed goes. He can swing the Bottle Man over to the brewery on Pile Street, and the Lady with the Fleas won't have to walk that long way to the Beauty Parlor.

Now there's commotion across the entire city, from Kikut to Nesodden. Herman looks around, pleased, and the morning becomes visible behind him, a weak, narrow hint of light down where the sky ends, or maybe begins.

Suddenly the door is opened wide. It hurts the eyes, and Herman turns toward the wall. But there is no wall there, just shadows and dust. He hears two hands clap together and a voice that steadily gets nearer and nearer.

"Oh, Herman, did you fall out of bed!"

He rises confused and sees that he's lying on the floor. Mother bends down to him, and then Father is there too, shirtless and with foam on his face.

"One sleeps best that way," Herman says, straightens his cap and lies down again.

They let him rest in peace. He doesn't have to go to the doctor until twelve o'clock. He hears the steps out to the kitchen and the radio holding devotions with organ and echo. Then he takes the cap off carefully, turns it inside out and looks for hair. He finds three strands. He puts them in the drawer along with the others. Then he feels his head all over, but doesn't come across any spots other than what he found yesterday. He takes a look around the room too, and only then does he discover that the globe has fallen from the windowsill during the night. It lies crushed under the radiator, in hundreds of world pieces, and the little light bulb inside is black and burned out. Then Herman remembers what he dreamed. He almost gets dizzy, and at the same time he remembers that this is the first time that he can remember a dream.

10.

MOTHER SITS UP STRAIGHT with her hands in her lap, breathing heavily and slowly. Father is there too. He has on a black suit he hasn't used since Christmas Eve. It's tight across the shoulders and much too short in the legs. In the middle is Herman, on a hard chair that sways. Behind them the nurse is sneezing powerfully. The doctor leans against the table, sniffles as if he's on the verge of tears, then looks up and dampens his lips with a big, red tongue.

He begins to speak without fastening his eyes anywhere.

"The tests we took confirm our suspicion, unfortunately. Herman has a hair disease which isn't dangerous in any way, but which leads to spotty hair loss, or in the worst case, he'll lose all his hair.

The doctor rises quickly and comes around the table.

"Now we must take off the cap, Herman."

"No."

"I can't see properly when you have it on, you know."

"You've seen enough."

Mother tries too.

"Take off the cap now, Herman. It's just us here."

Herman holds it tight with both hands. Father has to loosen his tie and his forehead is sweating.

"He can't help you if you have the cap on," Mother whispers.

"No one can help me."

The nurse comes forward, sneezes briefly, and bends down to Herman.

"Look at this. Do you want a marzipan chocolate?"

Herman lets go of the cap for a moment, and right then she snatches it from him, turns her back and sneezes again.

"That was a rotten trick," says Herman between his teeth.

"It isn't healthy to go around with a cap on all the time," explains the doctor, picking his nose. "It blocks evaporation from the scalp. Hair needs air! Tight fitting felt hats, kerchiefs and turbans can cause damage to hair growth. It's best to go bare-headed, Herman."

The nurse gives the cap to Mother and can't refrain from sneezing.

"I bet you gave it to each other," says Herman. "And I know how!"

Father drums with all his fingers on the armrest, and Mother lets out a short laugh which she swallows just as fast. The doctor turns red from his Adam's apple up. Then he gets out a magnifying glass and bends over Herman's head. It takes a long time, and his hands are more slimy than Egg's. It's like having hair full of snails. But suddenly he plucks out a hair. Herman screams and kicks him in the shin. The doctor limps back behind the table and wraps his nose in his hand-kerchief.

"The symptoms are obvious, unfortunately. Herman has already lost a spot, as you've certainly seen."

He holds up the little hair he stole.

"This is a so-called *club hair*, which grows around the bald spots."

"Club hair?" Mother asks.

"Yes, club hair. And club hair means that the disease is in progress. Do you understand what I'm saying, Herman?"

"I want my club hair back."

The doctor looks around a little bewildered, then reaches the little strand of hair across the table, and Herman puts it quickly in his pocket.

"But what's doing it?" Mother asks. "What's the cause?"

"That we don't know for certain. Some think it can be due to certain genes. Some think that anxiety is a contributing factor."

The doctor looks at Herman again.

"Is there anything you are nervous about, Herman? Anything particular that is bothering you?"

Herman doesn't answer.

"Something at school, for example? Something you've dreamed?"

Herman looks down and has a river behind each eye. It is so quiet that they can hear an eel twisting in the Atlantic Ocean. Mother comes with a hand that is almost transparent.

"You only have to say if you're nervous about something, Herman."

He raises his head and looks past the doctor, toward the windowsill.

"I'd rather not go up in the crane," he says softly.

Mother looks at Father, and Father's lips quiver.

"But you. . .you don't have to go. . .if you don't. . .want to. I can understand that, Herman. I just thought. . ."

He doesn't manage to say more and sinks down in his own lap. Herman doesn't dare look at him. The doctor gets out a bunch of papers. Mother sits on the edge of the chair.

"But isn't there anything we can do?"

"No, there really isn't. We must let it run it's course and let time take care of it. And don't believe those advertisements in the magazines. They're just gimmicks. Hair tonics and pomades do more harm than good."

"But how long will it take before. . ."

Mother closes her mouth and casts an eye on Herman.

"Before he eventually is bald? As I said, we know little. The hair can grow out again later, but I neither can nor will promise anything. The only thing I can suggest is a wig, when the time comes."

"Where's the plant?" Herman suddenly asks.

The doctor turns quickly to the windowsill, then he makes a crooked smile under his swollen nose.

"It died," he says.

On the way out Herman gets his cap back. He pulls it down tightly over his head and looks closely at the nurse. She has her name on a tag on her white coat.

"Did you sleep well last night in Homansbyen Cleaners?"

The nurse gets so confused that she sneezes four times in a row.

"You owe me a chocolate," is the last thing Herman says.

When they come out on the street, Herman is about to walk under a ladder. Mother pulls him around, and the three of them stop and look up. An old man who looks like a chimney sweep is changing the title on the sign over Frogner Theater. There is just one o left of *Zorro*. He pulls it down too and gets a new box of letters. They're smaller because the title is much longer. THE HUNCHBACK OF NOTRE DAME it says at last.

And in the snow on the sidewalk, Zorro lies mixed up. ROZOR. ORRZO. ZOROR. The man climbs down and puts the old letters in the box.

"Isn't there a new Zorro film coming?" Father asks.

"*The Hunchback of Notre Dame* is on the bill now, mister. With Charles Laughton. Not suitable for minors."

"But shouldn't there be a continuation of the Zorro film?"

"Sorry. The copy got destroyed during a robbery in the post office in New Mexico."

He takes the box under his arm and opens the door to the theater. Father stops him.

"But...how did it end?"

"They got away with a million dollars. Two postal workers were killed and four customers seriously injured."

"I mean with Zorro."

"Hmph. Don't really know. But he must have got the girl in the end. It usually goes like that."

The door shuts behind the old man, and Father turns toward Herman, shrugs his shoulders several times and doesn't know quite what to do. They stand there awhile searching for something to say to each other, but don't come up with anything, just like all the letters are changed around to make impossible words in strange languages in their mouths.

Father finally gets a sentence together in Norwegian.

"Here comes my streetcar!" he shouts, rushing over to the stop and hops on the second car. He waves three times, then they can't see him anymore.

Herman and Mother start to walk along Frogner Road. She pulls him away from the ladder again.

"It's bad luck to walk under a ladder," she says quickly.

"Bad luck's already happened," Herman says, kicking so hard in the snow that he stubs the asphalt.

"Don't talk like that," Mother pleads, squeezing his hand. "Guess what we're having for dinner?"

Herman twist his hand free and puts it in his pocket.

"Probably meatloaf with icky lumps in the gravy," he says.

Mother gives up. They walk a ways, each making tracks far from the other.

"I don't want a wig," Herman says quietly.

She comes closer again.

"It's not certain you'll need it either, you know. The doctor said that nothing was certain."

"Only girls use wigs. I'm not a girl."

Then he discovers Ruby. She's standing on the steps at Lille Frogner Avenue. She has seen him too. Around her head she has yellow ear muffs which push her red hair up in a huge clump. She follows him with her eyes and holds out her hand as if she can't decide whether to wave or not.

Herman looks every other direction, straightens his back and walks straight down Gabels Street. Mother has to speed up to stay with him.

"Wasn't that Ruby?" she asks.

"Who?"

"Ruby from your class?"

"One knows no Ruby."

"Ruby with the red hair?"

Herman refuses to answer anymore. He goes even faster and leaves Mother at least a block behind. She doesn't manage to catch up with him again until they are at Jacobsen's Groceries. She has to lean on Herman there and is almost out of breath.

"You can get out of going to Grandfather's today," she says finally.

"I don't want to get out of it."

Then she smiles a long time, gets the cardboard box for him, and Jacobsen Jr. holds the door for her and bows so deeply that he could eat his shoelaces.

"At your service, Mrs. Fulkt!"

He sees Herman, straightens up suddenly and puts his hands behind his back.

"Is it the squire Herman? Shall I drive you? In my Triumph?"

"One walks by himself."

Jacobsen Jr. pulls out a ballpoint pen from his breast pocket and holds it out.

"For you!"

"No, and that's final," says Herman taking the box and balancing it carefully through the streets as if he was holding a glass bowl with goldfish in it. He regrets not carrying Jacobsen Jr. away that night. He should have been stranded at Faerder lighthouse with only his cash register to row home in.

Grandfather lies in the canopy bed and has become even thinner and whiter. When he smiles, he has to lift the corners of his mouth with both hands. He smiles anyway. Herman sets the box on the night table and Grandfather climbs up on the pillow a little.

"Shall we see what it is today," he says and begins to unpack.

Herman finds a chair and watches Grandfather fill the bed with milk bottles, sausages, three hard-boiled eggs, half a loaf of bread, two raisin buns, a carrot and a can of mackerel in tomato sauce. But then he makes his eyes big and holds up a huge gold bar.

"Look at this, Herman. A marzipan chocolate! Now that's a surprise."

He tears the paper off at once, divides it in the middle

and gives Herman half.

"Let's eat it now. Even if it is between meals."

Grandfather gets a little color in his face and blends it out with a swallow of milk. Then he looks at Herman again and sinks down in the canopy bed.

"How is it outside now?"

"It's started to snow, Grandfather."

"Yes, I could feel it. That winter has come."

They don't say any more for a good while. Then Grandfather lifts his head from the pillow and smiles.

"There's an angel going through the room now," he whispers.

Herman looks around but doesn't see any angels, just dust floating across the floor. Are the angels dust? He has heard of some who have dust on the brain. Maybe that is dying?

Grandfather starts to laugh weakly down on the pillow, and the laughter is a thin thread.

"Don't let them bother you. The angels, I mean. They're okay for the most part."

"Who are the angels, Grandfather?"

"The angels. The angels are silence."

Herman thinks about that while a few angels are still wandering through he room. Then he moves the chair closer to the canopy bed.

"Grandfather?"

"I hear you, Herman."

"When did you lose your hair, Grandfather?"

"Oh, I started losing it in Turkey. During the World War, which I was in, you know. We were imprisoned in a cell underground. That was when I got high temples, as they say."

Grandfather feels his forehead and cracks open his eyes.

"It was worse for my friend, Waldemar. Waldemar was the captain of our battalion, and the Turks kept him in interrogation for forty days and forty nights. But Waldemar's mouth was shut with seven seals both in front and behind. At last they shot. But it didn't hit Waldemar. He had a blindfold on, you see, and a revolver against his temple. They shot someone else instead at the same time just to scare him, you know.

Waldemar didn't let himself scare so easily. But when he came back to the cell, he lost all his hair in the course of fifteen seconds. We used it as a pillow."

Herman gets restless on the chair.

"Did he lose all is hair in fifteen seconds?"

"He did. We counted."

"But how long did it take you, Grandfather?"

"It took me many years. And I haven't seen myself in a mirror since 1949."

Herman has to take a big gulp from the milk bottle.

"Wasn't there anything you could do?"

"About Waldemar? There wasn't anything. But let me tell you. Waldemar was really an archeologist."

"Arkologist. What's that?"

"An archeologist is someone who digs in the memory. After the war, Waldemar went to Egypt. There he found a little guy called Tutankhamen. He had been dead for three-thousand years. He was under a pyramid and was healthy as a fish, except for being dead. He was laying in a casket of gold, and do you know what Tutankhamen had on his head?"

Herman doesn't. He has to shake Grandfather's arm a little so he doesn't fall asleep.

"What did he have on his head, Grandfather?"

"The very finest wig. Only the pharaohs were allowed to use wigs in those days. Using a wig was considered a great honor."

Grandfather waves Herman closer with a curved finger.

"And this you must not tell a living soul, Herman. Waldemar just took that wig and used it the rest of his life."

Grandfather eats half a sausage and falls to sleep. Herman has to wake him.

"But what did you do?"

Grandfather looks around a little confused.

"Me? I drank beer."

It gets quiet on the pillow again, and Herman doesn't dare ask any more questions. He waits, and the angels come out from under the bed, and the clock in the corner ticks as if it's keeping rhythm to a soundless melody.

Grandfather rises up on his elbows and fastens his eyes on Herman.

"Nice cap you have."

"You drank beer?" Herman asks.

"You see, I read in a foreign newspaper that beer was good for hair. But I wasn't allowed to drink so much beer by Grandmother. Do you remember Grandmother, Herman?"

"She died before I was born."

"Shame. Grandmother was really very nice. But when it came to beer she was strict. Do you know what she said to me? I will not have a eunuch for a husband! Ha, ha."

Grandfather sinks down under the pillow with a little laughter in tow. An angel climbs up along the bedpost and disappears in the canopy sky.

"Should I pull the clock for you?" Herman asks.

He gets no answer. He goes over to the corner where it stands anyway, opens the narrow door and pulls the chain that the weight hangs on. It makes a nasty sound that gets Grandfather to move in the bed.

"Fine, Herman. It's running too slow."

"I thought it was running too fast," says Herman.

"Yes, well, it really doesn't matter."

Herman goes straight home. He stops outside the Bottle Man's window, but the shades are still down and there's not much sign of life. Then he makes up his mind, goes inside and finds the Bottle Man's door. There's a different name on the plate: Gøran Frantsén. Herman hesitates a little, then he rings. No one comes to open up. He rings again, and then he hears a low, rough voice far away.

"Who is it?"

Herman bends down and talks through the keyhole.

"It's Herman. The Claw."

"Climb on board, Claw."

The door is open, just like at Grandfather's, and Herman goes in. It is dark in all the rooms at the Bottle Man's. It smells like leftovers from last year, and he himself sits deep in a chair in the furthest corner. Herman glimpses empty bottles everywhere, and something is moving slowly across the floor, but he can't see what it is.

Suddenly the Bottle Man turns on a light. He has to shade his eyes, then he peeks at Herman between his fingers.

"Has the Christmas beer come?" he asks.

"Not yet."

Now Herman sees what's walking across the floor. It's a turtle.

"Don't be afraid. Its name is Time. Halt!" shouts the Bottle Man.

But the turtle just continues until it disappears under an escritoire.

The Bottle Man sighs and empties a bottle. Behind him, the corner is full of cobwebs; it looks like the safety net at a circus, but it hasn't helped the Bottle Man. He took his somersault and fell straight down long before the safety net was set up.

Herman takes a few steps closer and looks closely at the Bottle Man's head. His hair grows out in all directions and is thick as twine.

"You drink a lot of beer," Herman says.

The Bottle Man nods seriously.

"I'll soon have the verld's record. If I can just get enough beer."

He opens a new bottle and empties it right away. Herman almost thinks he can see the hair grow. The turtle sticks out his head for a moment and cranks it in again. The Bottle Man belches loud and long.

"I'm snow blind," he says. "I can't go out in the winter at all."

"I can buy beer for you, if you want," Herman says quickly.

The Bottle Man smiles widely without a single tooth in sight.

"That's it, Claw! Then maybe there'll be a verld's record this year. But remember to get a lettuce leaf. For Time."

Herman gets two bills and runs to Jacobsen's Groceries.

It's exactly closing time, and Mother has already gone home. Jacobsen Jr. is counting out the register and has green rubber caps on his fingers.

Herman puts the money on the counter.

"Beer and lettuce and make it quick," he says.

Jacobsen Jr. looks very suspiciously at him and straightens out the row of ballpoint pens in his breast pocket.

"And who is it for?"

"For the Bottle Man. Hurry up. He's going to set a world's record."

Jacobsen Jr. rolls his eyes, and no one can roll his eyes like him. His eyes almost take off in the air. Then he stacks the beer bottles in a box while he's looking another way, and places a wilted head of lettuce on the top.

Herman takes the goods in both arms, but Jacobsen Jr. doesn't bother to open the door for him. He remains standing behind the counter, fingering the bills.

"Tell him I'm keeping the change. Old and new debts."

Herman coaxes the door open with his left boot.

"The Bottle Man isn't good company for you. Herman. Keep away from him!"

"Keep away from my mother!" Herman says, kicking the door shut behind him.

Before he carries the box in to the Bottle Man, he takes out two beer bottles and hides them under the stairs. Then he goes in, and the Bottle Man is already prepared with the opener. He drinks three bottles at once and kicks the lettuce head over to the turtle.

"Chow time, Time!"

Herman looks at two photographs on the wall. The larger is of King Haakon. He didn't have much hair to brag about either, but then he surely never drank beer. Next to him hangs a picture of a lady with a huge hat on her head and a rose between her teeth. And that's all she's wearing.

"Is that the Belgian princess?" Herman asks.

The Bottle Man sets down the empty bottle and gets a sad form to his mouth—a cracked arch under his nose.

"Maybe it is," he mumbles into his beard stubble. "Maybe

it is. Yeah, that's probably the Belgian princess."

Then he turns out the lamp and sinks back in the chair under the cobwebs. Herman sneaks forward carefully, picks up the bottle opener and walks out backwards.

He sticks a beer bottle in each pocket, peeks around the corner, and the coast is clear. Then he runs across the street into the nearest yard, climbs over the fence, and there Herman sits down, behind a tree on the slope toward the railroad lines.

He opens the first bottle and takes a swallow. It immediately fizzes up his nose and spurts out from his entire face. It tasted worse than mushroom soup and cod-liver oil together, but maybe that's the intention. He tries a smaller sip, and this time it goes better. He's able to force it down. It burns behind his eyes and his stomach makes noise, a long growl. He relaxes a little, then takes another mouthful, gargles and swallows. He gets up quickly and sits down even faster. A train goes by, and he can barely see the tired faces behind yellow windows. The darkness is already beginning to fall from the sky. Frogner Inlet becomes one with Bygdøy, and the waves out on the fjord have white horns that butt and gore. The banana on the roof at Banan-Matthiessen looks like a peeled moon and the shadow of a cargo ship blows its horn by Dyna lighthouse.

Soon the bottle is empty. Herman takes the last mouthful, swallows hard and waits a minute, while the lights are lit at Oscar's Castle and the banana gets taken by the wind. Then he whips off the cap and feels with both hands. But he doesn't notice any difference. He gets close to the bare spot and pulls back his hands just as if he burned himself. It must take more beer. He opens the next bottle and gets right to the matter. He empties it over his head and rubs the beer in his hair thoroughly. Then Herman pulls on the cap and waits. He waits until the last train races by, but there are no faces to see on it, just empty windows and fluttering dark curtains.

Then Herman gets up and climbs the fence again. It's strange up in his head and he falls down on the other side.

He makes an angel in the snow when he first lies there then crawls on all fours and finds the street by way of many detours. He gets to his feet against a lamppost. There are internal gymnastics behind his forehead, and someone has turned the building he lives in upside-down. He lurches to the sidewalk across the street like a confused crab, finally running into the right entrance and clutching the banister. Now it's strange in both his head and his stomach, and the stair steps are so high and steep that he has to sit down and rest awhile. Then he hears a door open and voices he intends to recognize but can't go to the trouble. He has enough to think about. But suddenly a face comes into view. It resembles Mother's, except that Mother usually doesn't have four eyes and two heads.

It speaks from every direction.

"Herman? Are you sick, Herman?"

He doesn't manage to answer. His tongue weighs several kilos and soon won't fit in his mouth.

Now there are four heads approaching and just as many noses.

"Herman, have been drinking beer, Herman?"

It is silent for awhile, but there are no angels there anyway.

"Herman, are you a little tipsy?"

Then he remembers what Father usually does when he is going to do magic on Sundays. Herman raises his head with both hands and is about to stick a finger in his throat. But he doesn't reach it. He doesn't quite know what comes first, Mother's howl or his stomach. In any case, he must have thrown quite far because he can hear a solid splash all the way down on the first floor. Then there are only tears and pain and he feels arms lifting him up and more he doesn't know until he's sitting in the bathtub and Mother is trying to unscrew his head.

"It's frozen solid!" she shouts.

Father also has to grab hold. Herman isn't able to resist. He lets them hold on. Finally they get it, and Mother has the cap in her hand, twists it and sniffs. Afterward she's up in his hair.

"Herman, did you get beer on your hair too?"

"Hair tonic," Herman says.

He hears laughter, but not for long. Then the shower is turned on, and later he's in bed and is cold in the stomach and warm in the head. Mother takes a seat on the chair next to him and behind her stands Father. Then he discovers that the globe is in place on the windowsill again, and it glows stronger than ever. Herman points.

"Globe," he says.

"Dad bought a new one. Herman, where did you get the beer?"

"Stole it."

"Stole it? At Jacobsen's?"

"The Bottle Man."

"Was it the Bottle Man who gave you the idea? I mean, to put beer in your hair?"

"Tootin' common."

"Toot in common? What are you talking about now, Herman?"

"Did it help?"

"No, Herman. This kind of thing doesn't help at all. We just have to let time take care of it, like the doctor said."

Herman raises himself up in the bed, and for awhile he has four parents again. That's two too many.

"Who's Hugh?" he asks.

Mother's eyes get red.

"Hugh? Did you meet someone named Hugh, Herman?"

"Hugh, that Grandfather knew."

Mother is so relieved that she moves over to the edge of the bed.

"Did Father talk about someone named Hugh?"

"Hugh Nick."

Mother has to give up and change places with Father. He has something on his heart again, and his hands are big and clumsy.

"Herman, son? How ya doin' now?"

"No."

"That's understandable. It's no fun."

He looks out in space and the globe casts a strange light over half his face. Mother's thumbs are impatient.

"Thought I may as well buy a new globe," Father says.

"Thanks. Good-bye."

"It was nothing, you know. Have to have a globe so we know where we are."

Father is quiet for a long time.

"What I wanted to say, you know, Herman, that I thought about this here with the crane. Of course you don't have to go up. It's not that much to brag about anyway. Poor view too. Have you been awfully worried about it, Herman?"

"Don't remember."

"Let's say so, then. Think no more about it."

"No."

Father gets an idea.

"But we can go eel fishing, can't we?"

Herman pulls the comforter closer to his face.

"Whenever you say so."

"Agreed?"

Father smiles just barely in the globe's light and bends toward Herman.

He's already asleep.

11.

SOMETHING TICKLES HERMAN in the face. At first it's rather good. He chuckles in his sleep. Then it's no good any longer. It begins to itch inside his nose. It stings behind his forehead. It's almost like having a swarm of mosquitos in the mouth. He shadow boxes a little in the dark, but it doesn't help. Then Herman wakes from sneezing, a powerful trumpet blast that makes the globe rotate and the window shade roll up. The light from outside fills the room immediately. Herman sits up in bed and sees hair falling slowly towards the floor. He closes his eyes and feels his head carefully, first with just a single finger, then with both hands. He finds a new spot, right over the other ear, and still another in the front. Where is my cap? Herman thinks. *Where is my cap.*

He hears steps outside and hides under the comforter. The door opens and Mother peeks in.

"Herman? Are you there?"

"Here."

"Don't I get to see you?"

"My cap," he just says.

"I had to wash it, you know. Full of beer."

"Bring it here."

He sticks out a hand and gets a hold of the cap, pulls it down over his skull and folds the comforter aside.

"Hi, Herman. You haven't caught a cold?"

"No."

"You can stay home from school today anyway, if you want. It's already nine o'clock. Dad left for work a long time ago."

"Good for him."

"You remember what the doctor said about the cap?"

"No, and that's final."

Mother looks around the room, remaining quiet, picking up some strands of hair from the floor.

"Leave them alone!" Herman shouts.

She does what he says, standing still with her back to Herman awhile before she turns toward him.

"Did you lose a lot of hair tonight, Herman?"

He pulls the comforter back over himself.

"I'll never drink beer again."

"No, I don't suppose you will. It wasn't on account of the beer that you lost more hair, Herman."

Mother sits down on the edge of the bed and searches on top of the comforter with one hand. Herman pushes her away.

"And there isn't a thing we can do about it either. Except let time take care of it."

"Time is a turtle," Herman says.

"A turtle?"

"It eats lettuce and can't help me."

Mother thinks it over a long time, then stands up slowly.

"It's almost time for me to leave, now. Will you be alright alone, Herman?"

"Go your way."

"Breakfast's in the kitchen."

"Go your way."

"I can stay home if you want?"

"I'll manage."

"Of course, Herman. Okay, then. Bye."

She hesitates awhile.

"Bye?"

"Bye."

Then she goes her way. And that way goes down the stairs and around the corner to Jacobsen's Groceries. Herman waits until she's behind the counter weighing fish, then puts his feet in his slippers and sneaks around the apartment even though he knows no one else is there. It's strange. He can't remember being alone at home like this before. Everything suddenly looks different—the rooms are bigger, the light sharper. And it doesn't smell like usual; it smells of dust and tobacco. And it is so quiet, no radio, no voices, no plates breaking. Maybe he's not alone anyway. Maybe the angels are there right now? Herman stops in the living room and looks around. Even though Grandfather says they're okay, he doesn't like the angels playing hide-and-seek with him in silence. Maybe they are spies, spies from God?

He starts talking loudly to get rid of them.

"Ready or not, here I come! Ready or not, here I come!"

He listens, and right away he hears steps from the stairs. He goes to the window and waits. Two garbage men come out, each with a huge pail on the back.

"Serves them right," Herman says.

Then he sneaks further, to his parent's bedroom. He opens the door carefully, has to look over his shoulder to be completely certain no one sees him, and goes in. The double bed isn't made. The comforter has fallen down on the floor, and Father's polka dot pajamas lie on top of Mother's polka dot nightgown. Herman is going to move them, but changes his mind at the last second.

In the corner there's a table with an angled mirror that one can see oneself from all directions in, almost like the one Fats has in the window, only smaller. Herman hesitates, takes a step closer, pauses. He wants to run out, but can't. He closes his eyes and sits at the table with his head bowed and pulls off the cap. Then he raises his sight, and as he sees himself, right in front and in profile from both sides, he screams, and when he sees his own scream, he screams even louder. His hair hangs in clumps on his head. The bald spots stick out like white toadstools. He screams until the chair tips over. He tumbles backwards, but doesn't feel whether he hurt himself. He crab-runs across the floor, crawls through the apartment while he hears someone crying and doesn't realize it is himself. He finds the door to his room and goes in, pulls down the shade, turns off the globe and climbs under the comforter. There he remains, where it is darkest and no one cries any longer. He just hears his own voice, from all directions, as if it is the three-headed mirror that's talking.

"You are ugly. Herman, you are ugly, ugly, ugly, Herman. You're ugly!"

And the darkness gets blacker each time he says it:

"You're ugly, Herman. You're ugly!"

And from the eyes the darkness spreads into the entire body, a darkness that hurts, a darkness with shards of glass in it, broken mirrors and globes twisting and turning everywhere.

"I am ugly! I'm uglier. I'm the ugliest!"

And at last the darkness has taken all of Herman, with skin and what's left of his hair.

Then a strip of light becomes visible and another voice blends in.

"Are you still under the comforter, Herman?"

And farther away is yet another voice:

"Hasn't he eaten breakfast!"

Herman wraps the comforter tighter around himself and clamps his eyes shut.

"You don't have to hide from us."

The bed creaks when Mother sits down. Herman bites his teeth together, for in his mouth it's black too, so dark that his tongue will need a flashlight to speak clearly.

"Don't I get to see you, Herman?"

Mother tries to take away the comforter. Herman holds it in place. And the darkness makes him stronger than ever. He tears the comforter right out of Mother's hands.

Father's voice is nearby.

"I found his cap in the bedroom!"

He stomps in and comes to a quick stop.

"Here," Mother says.

She shoves the cap under the comforter to him.

"Did you go and look in the mirror, Herman?"

He isn't able to hold the darkness in his mouth any longer.

"Go away!"

Mother moves back and forth on the edge, as if she's sitting on a nettle.

"Guess what I bought for Children's Hour?"

"I don't care."

"Herman?"

"I don't give a shit!"

"Herman Fulkt?"

"Go away!"

It takes awhile, then he hears slow steps out of the room and the door being closed, quietly as an envelope.

Herman finds the cap in the dark, sticks his head in it and comes out of the comforter. He lights the globe, and America lights up the room. He listens, hears the radio, a voice talking about the weather. He folds the shade to the side. Soon it will be dark outside too. Snow is drifting and the streetlights are about to come on. He wishes that all the light bulbs in the entire city had burned out, that there was an eclipse, that the stars fell in the ocean, that the moon got a black patch over its eye.

Herman loosens the knot in his pajamas, and only now does he notice that he is soaking wet. He hides the bottoms under the bed and dries himself quickly on the comforter. Then he gets his clothes on at last and goes out in the hall and finds his boots and jacket.

Now Father's standing there.

"Where are you going, Herman?"

"No place."

"Where's that?"

"Anywhere."

Father doesn't know what to say. His head is so high he can almost scratch himself on the ceiling.

"But...but...what about *Stompa* on Children's Hour?"

"He can go pick his butt!"

Herman runs down the stairs. And he takes the other way when he comes out, to the left, where they can't see him from the windows.

He doesn't stop until he gets to Bygdøy Avenue. There the trees spread their arms like an army of scarecrows. Fats' place is dimly lit—maybe he's in there now, when all the customers have gone home, cutting his own hair? Herman runs up to Isachsen Sport and peeks in the window. The bicycles and soccer shoes are long gone. Speed skates are already in place. The shiny steel gleams. He pulls the cap even further down over his ears and pictures the blue ice, one arm on his back and one arm free, and he hears the roar from the turn when he leans over, speeds up onto the straightaway and crosses to the inner lane with at least a ten meter lead.

Then there is another sound instead, coming from down Frogner Road and coming closer. It's singing in loud and out-of-tune voices. Herman hunches up in the entrance and sees Glenn, Karsten and Bjørnar running along the streetcar tracks hollering: "There's a hole in the fence at Gaustad. There's a hole in the fence at Gaustad. There's a hole in the fence at Gaustad, and that's why we're here!"

Herman waits until they're out of sight and the song is just an echo between the buildings where the curtains are being drawn in all the windows and shadows dance slowly to music from invisible orchestras. Then he takes the short cut to Frogner Theater. There's a line on the sidewalk outside. The seven o'clock show is about to begin. Herman looks at the pictures first, and then he almost screams again. He has to close his eyes, but it doesn't help at all. It gets worse, for inside him it's also full of frightening pictures. I'm just as ugly, he thinks, as ugly as the Hunchback of Notre Dame. He doesn't want to, but can't stop looking anyway. The Hunchback of Notre Dame has barely one eye, his mouth is a crooked hole, his nose points straight up, and his head is so huge it barely fits on the hunched back. And the hair, his hair is thin and transparent and hangs in clumps on his dented skull. But in one of the pictures there's a lady too, and she is so pretty she is almost invisible. And the Hunchback of Notre Dame holds her, and it doesn't look like she particularly minds it either. Herman stands there a long time wondering about that particular picture. Then he gets in line, and the door opens. But when it's his turn, a heavy arm falls in front of him and blocks the way. Herman looks up. It's the same old man who was hanging the letters on the sign. Now he has a uniform with stripes and buttons on and is an usher.

"Where do you think you're going?"

"To the movie," Herman answers.

"It's a grown-ups film tonight."

"I don't mind."

"Are you with someone, maybe?"

"Not that I know."

The usher is beginning to get impatient.

"And how old do you expect me to believe you are?"

"I am a very old man," says Herman.

With that he gets maneuvered out of line, and soon he's the only one left on the sidewalk. The usher closes the doors and the fanfare starts up inside the auditorium. Herman has to look at the picture of the Hunchback one more time, but then he catches sight of a swaying figure over by the streetcar tracks. He sees at once that it's the Lady with the Fleas. She's struggling forward as she can, and it's not so much. And there must be a lot of fleas tonight; her body makes big tosses in all directions and her head sits loosely.

"It hasn't begun yet!" Herman calls. "It's still just the commercials!"

He doesn't know whether she can hear him. In any case she tries to run, stumbles on her impossible legs, gets up on her crutches again, totters farther, and she makes it, at the last second, but she makes it.

For a moment she looks over at Herman, a strange look, as if they share a secret.

Then the Lady with the Fleas slips in, and the church bell rings, far away, in the auditorium's blue darkness.

When Herman gets home, a new pair of pajamas lie on his bed, with red polka dots. And the comforter cover is changed. It smells of detergent and wind. He peeks under the bed. The wet pajama bottoms are gone.

Then he takes out the herbarium, finds a tube of Karlson in the drawer, and glues in all the hairs he has kept hidden. And the very littlest hair gets a whole page to itself.

Underneath he writes with a pencil in block letters:

Club hair. Found on Herman Fulkt's head.

12.

HERMAN STANDS IN THE KITCHEN, his school bag packed, his cap pulled down in front, and is ready.

"I'm going to school."

His parents look at each other first, then both look at him.

"It's Sunday today," Mother says.

Herman is a little confused, and only then does he discover the eggs, teapot and toast on the table.

"Then school is closed," he mumbles and twists off his bag.

Father is in a good mood and is already busy making a huge lunch.

"Today we're going eel fishing, Herman! What do you say to that!"

Herman sits down and has no appetite.

"Sure," he says.

"A big, fat eel that we can save for Christmas. It'll be time for aquavit!"

Mother looks at Herman, and Herman looks out the window. He should have seen at once that it was Sunday. No other day has the same color as Sunday. It is gray, gray as the hymns on the Request Concert.

"But maybe he doesn't want to go fishing for eel?"

Father turns to Mother astonished.

"Doesn't want to? Of course he wants to! Don't you, Herman?"

Herman tries to look Father in the eyes.

"Of course."

"I thought that he might want to go to Grandfather's with me instead."

"But you heard what he said. Besides, I'll need help carrying all the eel home. How much bread do you want, Herman?"

"A half one."

Father is still laughing as they walk down toward the dock. He laughs so the rucksack shakes and it sounds quite good, for in it he has a big nail and two empty cans with line around them and hooks.

"A half one! You're quite a joker, Herman!"

Herman doesn't say anything. He has more than enough to do just keeping up. When Father takes one step, Herman must take at least four. And the streets are sad and go the wrong way. Sunday Morning is the most lonesome of all mornings. It was then that God overslept and forgot to set the world in motion. The only ones out now, except for Herman and his father, are some dark, slow figures far away who are on their way to some church or other in order to wind the world's alarm clock so that God will wake up, part the clouds, light the sun, and make new plans that they hope will be better than the old ones.

"Soon now you'll get to meet a couple of my sidekicks, Herman. Bock and Rags are sure to be there. Bock got a huge one in '59. It was big as a boa constrictor, I swear. He flayed it and used the skin for a tent the next summer!"

Father stops and looks restlessly down at Herman.

"I guess I'm exaggerating a little," he says.

But there's no one else at Fred Olsen Wharf. The waves are black and roll slowly toward the pillars. A cargo ship rocks farther away, and the wind gets sound out of a rusty cable.

Father looks around.

"They'll show up, Bock and Rags. Lucky anyway. Now we'll get the best spot!"

And that's where the sewer comes out. Father takes out the two cans and shows how they work. He swings the line like a lasso three times around his head, releases, and the hook disappears in a high arc, lands with a plunk, and sinks right down to the eels. When Herman is going to cast, the hook lands between some boxes on the other side of the road.

"Good distance, Herman. Next time you'll hit Oslo Fjord!"

He tries again, swings the line around and around. Father counts to three and shouts let go! Herman opens his hand and the hook plops right down in the water.

"Let out some line! It's fine right there!"

Then they sit down on the edge of the dock and wait. Nothing happens. Herman's happy about that. But maybe an eel is right now on it's way past Dyna lighthouse. Maybe it has swum for several years in order to get so far, and now it's approaching, down there in the dark, and of all the hooks in the seven seas it's going to bite Herman's.

It can't be possible.

"When you're going to skin an eel, you know, Herman, you have to make a cut around it's throat, and then you hold it tight by the head and pull the skin off. Almost like a sausage. And presto, right into the kettle with it. And whatever's left over we put in the soufflé.

Father lets out more line and sets down the can.

"I'm getting hungry, by God. How about a sandwich, Herman?"

"I'm not really hungry."

"Not even a half one?"

Father has to laugh again. He unwraps the lunch, rubs his hand on his pant legs a long time and munches away.

"Have you stuck your finger in your throat today?" Herman asks.

"Have I what?"

Father gets bologna caught crosswise in his throat, and Herman pounds away on his back to get it out.

"That was close," he pants and throws the sandwich out in the water. "Thank you."

Herman sits down by the can again and wraps the line around his thumb. Father lights a cigarette and makes blue clouds around his face. And that's the way they remain sitting, while the wind turns and comes from behind instead and the alarm clocks ring at the same time in all the city's churches.

"Didn't stick my finger in my throat today. It wasn't necessary, you know."

They don't say any more for awhile. Then Father says: "You know what?"

"No."

"Me neither."

He pulls in the line and throws it out again.

"Strange that Bock and Rags haven't come yet," Father says quietly.

Herman peeks over at him carefully.

"Do you have a lot of friends, Father?"

Father stares out at the fjord, which lies black and shiny now, reflecting the restless sky.

"There's you and Mom, you know. Bock and Rags are just some people I know. I'm not sure they're coming either. It's getting late in the season. It's winter already."

"Yes. It is winter now," Herman says.

Then his finger suddenly jerks, and the line is taut down in the water. Herman almost tips over. His back freezes. He thinks about the eel down there, swimming through seven seas in order to end up in a soufflé, the slimy eel in the sewer, and he can't handle that thought. Father hasn't noticed anything. Herman's thumb is about to come off. And then he does it, almost without knowing that he's doing it, but he wonders if he'll have a guilty conscience anyway. Herman presses the line as hard as possible against the edge of the tin can and the line breaks with the same sound as an out of tune guitar string.

Father is already up. Herman gets to his feet too.

"I had one! It broke the line right off."

He shows the can.

"Did it break the line!"

Father is shouting.

"It broke the line!"

"It must have been gigantic! It's never happened before!

Did it just snap the line in two?"

"It pulled, tugged, and then the line broke!"

"Wow, Herman."

"Yeah, wow. It must have been huge."

"Did you see it?"

"Didn't have time."

"I've got to have a sandwich, Herman!"

Later, they walk home with an empty rucksack and one less hook. The season is over. They pass the construction site at Vika, and both slow down. The crane hangs down from the clouds and barely reaches the ground. Father is about to say something, but doesn't anyway. Herman also has something he'd like to have said, but doesn't either.

So they walk silently the last bit, each with his thoughts, through quiet streets that smell of Sunday dinners and black coffee.

But at last Father says:

"Must have been a really huge one, Herman. A lot bigger than the one Bock got in '59."

13.

HERMAN DOESN'T WANT TO. Herman doesn't want to go. Herman doesn't want to go to Fats'. He holds tight to the chair and refuses to leave the room. Mother stands in the doorway and has already put on her coat.

"But there's nothing to be afraid of. You've been to Fats' many, many times."

"I don't want a wig!"

"He's just going to measure, Herman."

"You won't trick me again!"

Mother takes two steps into the room and is about to twist a button off.

"I've never tried to trick you. You know that, Herman. Fats is just going to look at your head so he can make a hairpiece in case you might have a use for it some day. Okay?"

She looks right at Herman and something dawns on her. She quietly says:

"Is it because you don't want to take off the cap?"

Herman makes a nod and stares down at the floor.

"Fats has seen all kinds of hair, Herman. That's his job. He's seen hair that grows inward and ladies with beards and moustaches."

"Doesn't help."

"Fats has a private room behind the salon where no one else can see us."

"Doesn't help either."

"We can go to Studenten for ice cream afterwards."

Herman wrinkles his forehead.

"And eat banana splits. With chocolate sauce and red currant jam."

Herman listens.

"And raspberry milkshakes."

Herman thinks it over well.

"When you put it like that," Herman says.

He walks as slowly as he can up Gables Street pretending there's glue under his boots. But no matter how slowly he walks, he finally gets there. It's really quite strange when you think about it.

Fats is ready at the door. He has a new, chalk-white coat on, with two combs and one pair of scissors in the breast pocket. His black moustache glistens under his nose, and he bows even deeper than Jacobsen Jr. and rises slowly with a big, red face on top.

"This way!"

They are led through the shop where old men have fallen asleep in the chairs and the same ladies with helmets on their heads sit knitting potholders. Fats opens yet another door and they come to a new room. There's a barber chair in front of a wall that isn't a wall but a gigantic mirror.

"Welcome!"

Fats closes the door, rubs his hands and circles around Herman several times.

"Shall we sit down?"

"You first."

Fats looks at Mother and laughs loudly. Then he puts his hand on Herman's shoulder and stops laughing.

"I meant you."

"I don't want to look in the mirror."

"Don't you want to see the mirror?"

He turns toward Mother again. She makes several motions and Fats smiles so wide that the moustache almost breaks.

"Alright, Herman. We just have to turn the chair.

He loosens a lever and spins the barber chair the other

way. Herman climbs up and sits, and Fats pumps on the pedal as if he were in a bicycle race. He has to lower Herman back down before they are at head height.

"And let's take off our cap."

"You don't have a cap," Herman says.

Fats turns red, but it isn't easy to see, for he's quite pink already. The moustache gets restless under his nose.

"I meant you."

Herman closes his eyes for safety's sake and pulls off the cap. He can feel Fats' heavy breath from all directions and fingers that come in close contact.

"And how would you like it today?"

"I don't have a brother!"

Herman opens his eyes and Fats looks down.

"Am I saying stupid things today, Herman?"

"Yes."

It is quiet a long time. Mother has taken off her coat and sits on a spindly chair by the door and doesn't know out from in. She tries to smile, but the smile gets crosswise in her mouth.

"Think I'll have an ice cream float too," she says softly.

Fats has taken out a measuring tape. He leans over Herman and turns his head from side to side.

"This looks good, Herman."

"It doesn't look good at all."

"Sure, you've lost a little hair here and there. But your head is top-notch. Perfect shape. Made to order, if I may say so. Did I say something stupid again?"

"Yes."

Then Fats begins to measure. He measures from ear to ear, from the forehead to the neck, from temple to temple, from the part to the crown, across and around, taking notes on a pad the whole time while he sweats a lot and hums "Tango For Two." Finally he clips off a lock and puts it in a transparent bag.

Fats is pleased.

"This will be fine, Herman. No one will be able to tell the difference."

Herman pulls his cap in place and Mother stands up.
"Add a centimeter," she says. "So he can grow in it."
"Of course. Besides, they're very elastic."
Now Fats looks at Herman again.
"I don't suppose you want buffalo hair? Or goat hair? No, of course not. We use the finest European hair. You won't recognize yourself. I mean, you'll look better than ever! And you don't have to get your hair cut with me anymore! What do you say to that, Herman?"
"Who cuts your hair?"
Fats sticks the scissors in his breast pocket and down-pedals the chair.
"My mother," he says quietly. "She's eighty-one. But I do the moustache myself."
He suddenly gets busy with some drawers.
"It takes some time to make a natural-hair wig. It's an art, if I may say so myself. Vigelands Park wasn't built in a day, by comparison. But you'll get it in plenty of time. There's still hair left. I'd say December."
Fats has finally found what he's looking for. He unwraps a box, folds aside the paper, and with proud hands lifts out a scalp.
"But in the meantime, while you're waiting for your European wig, this is yours!"
He hands the scalp ceremoniously to Herman, who sends it directly on to Mother. She holds it as if she has just gotten an eel and has no idea how to kill it. But at least the scalp isn't wiggling. It's completely still.
"Direct from Korea," Fats continues. "Synthetic, it's called. Quite useful, and better than nothing."
He looks quickly at Herman and strikes his thumb along his moustache. Then it isn't black any longer, but almost yellow. He wipes his fingers on the coat, which becomes full of dark spots.
"But aren't you going to try it!" he shouts.
Herman is already on the way out. Mother throws on her coat, puts the scalp in her purse and follows him.
"And it doesn't take heat well," says Fats. He sits down in

the barber chair and begins to color his moustache.

Herman waits behind a chestnut tree without chestnuts. Mother finds him there, while he stares up between the branches and sees the clouds gather into more snow.

"Aren't we going to Studenten?" she asks.

"Who cares," Herman says, shaking his cap.

Mother takes a better grip of her purse and speaks so softly that his ears need to strain.

"Are you mad, Herman?"

Herman kicks the tree three times.

"Don't know. Maybe soon."

That evening he tries the wig. He sits in his room, takes off the cap and places the wig carefully on his head. It's tight around the neck and forehead and itches by both ears. But maybe that's the intention. And when he runs his fingers through the new hair, he just about gets shocked. He paces back and forth a little and feels it properly. It's a strange feeling. It's just as if it isn't him walking there between the door and the window, but a cousin, and Herman has no cousins. His head is heavy and unwieldy, and he wonders if his voice has also been changed. Korea, he says aloud, but can't hear anything different so far. Korea! Then he finds Korea on the globe, and it's really not so strange that they make wigs there, since Korea is almost on the other side of the world, and they probably have to walk on their heads there.

Herman hurries to his parents in the living room. He wonders whether they'll recognize him. At first, he's in doubt because they look mostly at each other.

"Herman here," he says softly, and now his voice has been changed too. It sounds like a poorly tuned radio. Maybe he's going to start speaking Korean soon?

Finally, Mother gets up and comes to him.

"Splendid, Herman. You look splendid."

"Really?"

Father thinks so too.

"Wonderful! Almost wish I had one myself."

"Maybe you can borrow it," says Herman, beginning to get his voice tuned in again.

"But it's probably better if you don't have it backwards."

Mother takes hold by the ears and turns the wig around. Then it's not tight at the forehead any longer, but itches in the neck instead.

"Wow, Herman. Now you really look fine!"

Father talks loud and grating as if he, too, is a radio.

Herman takes a few quick steps around the living room, gets a little dizzy and has to lean against the wall.

"Is everything alright, Herman?" Mother asks.

"I'm just breaking it in."

"Shall we look in the mirror?"

Herman hesitates.

"I'll sleep on it first."

14.

HERMAN STANDS IN THE HALL outside the classroom and waits. It's cold and quiet, smells of old lunch bags and dried sponges. He reads through the science lesson and pictures the innards of cows and wonders how green grass can turn into milk with cream in it. Rødkolle and Telemarksfe cattle, he studies. Then he hears rapid footsteps echoing from all directions. He looks around. It's the cleaning lady coming up the stairs. She sets down the broom and pail and examines him.

"Hi, Herman. Early bird today?"

"Yeah."

"Are you supposed to be here? Before the bell rings?"

"Haven't asked."

"That's good, Herman."

The cleaning lady smiles a long time. Then she takes her equipment and walks down the corridor. Herman thinks it over thoroughly two times, then runs after her.

"Can you let me into the classroom?"

She stops and leans on the broom.

"I don't know if I'm allowed to."

"Have you asked?"

Then she pulls out a huge bunch of keys and unlocks the door.

"Are we done now, Herman?"

He turns toward her.

"How did you know my name?"

The cleaning lady is suddenly embarrassed, makes a huge lower lip and blows the hair away from her face.

"Isn't your name Herman?"

"Yes. Has everyone been talking about me?"

"Woody told me your name," she says quickly and disappears down the hall.

Herman closes the door and sits down at his desk in the window row. The schoolyard is still empty. The chalkboard is black as a window in the night, and on the teacher's desk is a new box of chalk. It's exactly as if everything is waiting to be put to use, the inkwells for pen points, the trash pails for waste, and this waiting time is like a dream or a promise.

Herman discovers something on Ruby's desk. He leans forward and sees that it's an H, an H carved into the top. Herman falls back in his chair and ponders it. An H. It could be H for King Haakon, or Crown Prince Harold. It could be H for Hamar, health or Huckleberry Hound. It could be H for anything from hammock, hangar and Holland to hurrah. Herman lets it rest at that and takes out his workbook. Barrel isn't going to stump him today. Herman writes: *The cow swallows the grass without chewing it. The cow's stomach is divided into four parts. First the food glides in a big sack, the rumen. From there it goes into the reticulum. When the cow rests it regurgitates it up in the mouth and fine chews it. The fine chewed food glides down in the omassum. From there out in the abomasum.*

Barrel is suddenly at the door. He looks at Herman, surprised, starts to say something, but isn't fast enough.

"Wasn't locked," Herman says, snapping his workbook closed.

Barrel takes awhile to find the right words.

"Nice that you're not late, Herman. That's the way it should be. That's the way it should be, alright."

Barrel sits down heavily behind his desk. Finally the bell rings, and soon the entire class comes storming in a huge mob. But when they see Herman, they get quiet as angels and dust and find their places without a sound, not even a chair scraping along the floor. Not even Glenn makes noise today, and Ruby sits with her neck bowed and rummages in her school bag. H, Herman thinks. H for Holmenkollen and hula hoop.

Barrel begins immediately to draw a cow's stomach on the board. It takes quite a long time, and looks at last like an unsuccessful pretzel.

"And what is this stomach called?"

Herman shoots his arm in the air, but Barrel asks Glenn instead.

"Rum."

"Wrong, you goof-off."

Herman shakes his hand and sticks out his fingers, but it's just as if Barrel doesn't see him.

"Bjønar! Answer!"

"Abomasim."

"You lunkhead! Karsten, did you hear what I asked!"

"Udder."

Barrel gets a sad expression in his eyes and Herman has almost gotten out of his chair. But that doesn't help either. Now Ruby is called to the board, and she writes all the names where they belong. Herman could have done it even faster. He lets down his arm and waits for the next question. Then it goes to the top again.

"Name three different varieties of cattle!"

But Barrel doesn't catch sight of Herman this time either. Ruby is still standing at the chalkboard.

"Dølafe, Telemarksfe and rødkolle," she answers. "Rødkolle is the only one that doesn't have a horn."

"Good!" Barrel shouts.

"And trønderfe," Herman says to himself.

Ruby goes back to her desk while Barrel draws the outline of a cow's head next to all the stomachs. Then Herman starts to feel warm. He's sitting next to the radiator. It's soon so warm that his head is going to melt like an ice cream cone. It itches at the neck and is tight at the temples. It prickles in the forehead and pinches above the ears. It's just like he's packed full of prickly rose hips and black pepper.

Herman takes off his cap.

A deep sigh goes through the class, a long gasp. Ruby turns and lifts her hand to her mouth, as if she has to hold it in place. Then it becomes even quieter than before, so quiet they can hear a snowflake land on an evergreen needle in Valdres. Barrel does an about-face, fastens his eyes right on Herman's wig and drops the chalk to the floor. It sounds like a bomb blast. Barrel smiles helplessly and uses the rest of the hour to tell about the difference between sheep and goats at a furious pace.

Herman slowly pulls on his cap again and stares out the window while he thinks about the gnawing tooth of time, as some people say. It's really a bit strange that time only has one tooth, but time must be very old, having been up since the dawn of time. Herman tries to imagine such a smile: Time, grinning with one rotten tooth pointing down in front. It isn't a very pleasant picture.

At recess he stands alone by the drinking fountain. And again it's just as if he were invisible; they all look past him, turn their eyes down and pull away. No one attempts to pull off his cap. No one makes fun of him. It almost would have been better if they had. Then he could at least have defended himself and threatened them with club hair. Now he doesn't have anything to be involved in. Herman begins to understand something, but doesn't quite know what it is he understands. They feel sorry for me, he thinks. And that's about the worst thing possible.

And so the day continues. Everyone is silent as a clam. Everyone moves in big circles around him, something happening behind his back the whole time. Something, he doesn't know what. But he begins to understand more and more. They only feel sorry for me, Herman thinks again. Even Woody comes to class on time and doesn't mention a word about the herbarium. He leaves Herman alone at a table with nothing to do there. He cuts out three round cardboard figures which he tosses away when the bell rings.

But in the last class, gym, Herman understands the most.

Egg is completely soft-boiled and doesn't see Herman either even though he hasn't changed and keeps his cap on. Egg climbs up the stall bars and hangs there by one hand.

"Spirit in the breast, sweat on the forehead, and last but not least, steel in the legs and arms!" he shouts. "Today is penance and prayer, my dear boys. Therefore I've decided that you're going to play cannonball!"

Egg has never gotten so much applause. Two benches are placed end-to-end in the middle of the floor, and Glenn and Bjønar get to choose teams. Glenn is eager, and then the first thing happens that makes Herman understand that they are afraid of him too, because they feel sorry for him.

Glenn looks around the gym, eyes wavering, and it's the only time anyone has seen him turn red.

Glenn points but looks another direction.

"Herman," he says weakly.

The teams line up on each side of the benches. Egg tosses the ball to Bjørnar, climbs up the stall bars again and hollers:

"Only throws with both hands over your head are allowed! No aiming at the face and other protruding body parts. Understand!"

Then he blows the whistle, walks over to Bjørnar's side, and the battle is underway. Glenn propels the ball right in Karsten's stomach, and Bjørnar kicks it back in the middle of Glenn's shorts. One by one they are hit and have to go behind the line. Herman runs in zig-zags, but no one aims at him anyway, since he's invisible again. He could just as well have stood completely still, and the balls would swish by on all sides but never hit. At last only Herman and Egg are left. Egg walks toward the bench, lifts the ball over his head, and Herman can see it already, before Egg throws, that he's going to miss on purpose. The ball hits the floor without Herman moving the width of a comma. Glenn pushes the ball out to him. Herman takes it, walks slowly toward Egg, whose upper body makes many strange motions. Herman aims painstakingly, throws as hard as he can, and a flat slap is heard when the ball hits Egg in the middle of the face.

"Great throw," whispers Egg, tottering along the wall of

stall bars.

And at the same time Herman understands that he has won and still lost.

He turns his back to the sound of stamping feet, gets his jacket from the locker room, runs up the stairs, but is stopped by Barrel there.

"You're just who I'm looking for," Barrel says.

"You found me," Herman says, trying to get past.

Barrel stops him with one finger.

"The bell hasn't rung yet. Stay with me."

"Is this detention?"

They walk together across the school yard to the other building. Barrel unlocks the classroom door and sits at one of the desks. It's much too small for him. He looks like an elephant in a baby carriage. He suddenly looks very sad.

"I've never held anyone out the window by the ear, Herman. It's just a story."

"Omassum," Herman says.

"Excuse me?"

"Reticulum and abomasum."

Barrel smiles.

"Stories like that get started, and then people start to believe them. You don't believe it, do you, Herman?"

"Rødkolle, telemarksfe, dølafe and trønderfe."

"Good, Herman."

"From cows we get milk and leather."

"What I wanted to say. . ."

"From milk we make cream, cheese and butter."

"Fine, Herman. You've done your homework, I see."

"Can you see me now?"

Barrel's ears turn red and flap like two flounders.

"I see you, Herman. I understand."

"Sheep have round bodies and thin legs. Goats have thin bodies and beards. But we butcher both."

"You've read more than your lesson, I see. The way it should be. What I wanted to say, Herman. I have something for you."

He pulls something up from his coat pocket and wants

to give it to Herman. It takes awhile before he sees what it is. It's the tassel Barrel tore off.

"I'm sure your mother can sew it back on."

"No," Herman says.

Barrel is confused.

"No? But I'm sure she can."

"No. You can just throw it away."

Barrel puts the tassel down on the desk and his face gets even sadder.

"You don't want it then?"

"No. Use it yourself."

The bell rings. Herman takes a step toward the door. Barrel gets up and has to lift his stomach at the same time with both hands even though he has double suspenders.

"But you don't believe that story, do you?"

Herman doesn't want to be there any longer.

"No, and that's final."

Then he spurts down the corridor and out to the schoolyard, which is already empty, as if everyone has fled at breakneck speed, as if he were the world champion infection carrier. But Herman knows better. He knows better now. He knows that they let him win, and that's worse than losing. He knows that they feel sorry for him, and so they're suddenly nice or gone. He doesn't quite know whether he wants to know this, but it's too late; he knows already.

He hears someone whistling. He turns around. Ruby is standing at the gate at Holtesvingen, waving at him. Herman is so surprised that he stumbles a few steps in the snow. He finds his balance. She keeps waving, and he remains in the same place. Now it's her turn. She comes toward him, earmuffs, red hair, pink school bag. H, Herman thinks. H for Hopalong. H for hair. Suddenly he sticks out his tongue. It sort of falls out of his mouth and points at her. Ruby looks bewildered at first, and two dimples dig in her face. Then she stops, stares at Herman's tongue, and doesn't smile at all any longer.

Herman snaps around and runs to the other gate, to Harelabben. There he slows down and looks over his shoulder. She isn't following him. He only sees her back as she disappears around the corner. And Herman continues slowly down Briskeby Road, turns now and then, but Ruby isn't there, and he doesn't quite know whether he should be pleased with himself.

15.

HERMAN PUSHES THE DOOR open, senses the closed in, slightly sickly air and hears the clock strike three. He walks into the room and Grandfather is still lying as he has nested. He's sleeping, and his head doesn't even make a dent in the pillow. Herman sits down on the chair by the bed and doesn't want to wake him. He takes off his cap and wonders whether Grandfather has plenty of time or not enough right now.

Then he sees a photograph that has fallen down on the floor. He picks it up. It's of Grandmother. She's standing under the apple tree at Nesodden long ago and has an umbrella even though the sun is shining.

"Life is a shoelace."

Herman lets go of the picture and moves the chair closer to the bed.

"Life is a shoelace," Grandfather repeats, opening his eyes. "I don't think I'll go skiing today either, Herman."

They both laugh awhile, then an angel comes and Herman feels he must say something.

"Do you see the difference?" he asks.

Grandfather turns his head in the right direction.

"Difference? Have you sent a double?"

"No. I am me."

"That's good to hear. You are you."

"Grandfather is Grandfather."

"I can promise you that. And Herman is Herman. I think there's more chocolate."

He finds a piece, but isn't able to break it in two. Herman has to help him finally. They each suck their own bit a long time.

"Were you in love with Grandmother?" Herman asks.

"Like a bull."

Grandfather swallows the chocolate, thinks about it.

"Not just like a bull. Do you know how I met Grandmother?"

Herman doesn't know.

"I was tying my shoelaces."

"Shoelaces?"

"That's what I said, Herman. Shoelaces. I was going to Nesodden, but in the middle of City Hall Square the knot in my right shoe came loose. This was in May, 1920, you see. And so I had to tie it, but then I didn't get to the boat on time, ten thirty-five, and had to wait for the next one, which departed an hour later. Anyway, it was the *Flaskebekk*. It sank in the Indian Ocean in 1949. But everyone survived. Are you breaking off another bit?"

Herman does, and has to wait until Grandfather has sucked the chocolate soft.

"And on board the *Flaskebekk,* on deck, I met Else Marie Louise, who was going to be your Grandmother, Herman. She came all the way from Nittedal and was visiting the city to visit a friend who had moved to Ildjernet. She got off at Nesoddtangen, and I didn't let her out of my sight. That's how it was, Herman. If my shoelace hadn't broken, you wouldn't be here. I still have it, but the shoes are probably gone."

"But who is Hugh Nick, Grandfather?"

"Hugh Nick, did you say?"

"Hugh Nick that Grandmother didn't want for a husband. When you drank beer."

Grandfather gets a wrinkle crosswise around his entire head. Then he smiles weakly.

"Eunuch, he's called. Eunuchs are men who never lose their hair. And girls don't particularly like that."

"Girls don't like that, Grandfather?"

"They like good skulls."

"Do they?"

"What do you think Else Marie Louise fell for on board the *Flaskebekk* in 1920? My head, first and foremost."

Herman has to think hard about that.

"Is Dad a eunuck?"

Now Grandfather is starting to get tired out.

"Dad isn't a eunuch. He proved that long ago."

"Proved it how?"

"Mom wanted him. And you are the proof. It's a shame that Grandmother died before you were born, Herman. Do you know how she died? She tripped in the gutter when we were running across City Hall Square to get the Nesodden boat one Saturday in 1949. God is a funny guy."

"Do you believe that?" Herman asks.

Grandfather sighs a little.

"Not really. Anyway, have I told you about the time I fell from the ladder with a bucket of paint in each hand?"

"I think so."

"I had to get the house at Nesodden in shape for the next time Else Marie Louise came there. And this was the same day she was going to come, you know. One color was white and the other was black. I looked like a zebra, and this wasn't the kind of paint you can get off in a jiffy. But did I put off meeting her because of it? Oh, no. I was standing at the dock when the boat came and carried her up the gangplank. And Else Marie Louise took me as I was."

Grandfather closes his eyes and sleeps. His face becomes smooth and transparent again. Herman sits a long time looking at him. He doesn't quite know whether he should do what he has in mind, but does it anyway. He twists the wig; it hangs on. It's like tearing off a band-aid. Then he lays it carefully on Grandfather's head. It doesn't look so good. It looks like an old pancake with streaks in it. It looks like a cow turd with bristles. It looks like a kettle lid with quills. Herman lifts up the wig, stuffs it in the bottom of his school bag and puts on his cap. Then something comes to him. He puts the photograph of Grandmother in Grandfather's slender, blue hand.

Herman sneaks out, but before he gets to the door he hears a little sound from the canopy bed. He turns, sees that Grandfather is smiling, laying his other hand up on the picture too, so no one can take it from him.

16.

HERMAN SITS IN THE BATHTUB with his back arched, biting his teeth together and holding a wet cloth in front of his eyes. Mother squirts thick gunk, which resembles Woody's glue, over his head and rubs it gently in what's left of his hair. In the living room, the radio sobs in foreign languages, and now Mother whips cream instead, which runs past Herman's face in great quantities.

"Shampoo," she says.

"Me neither," Herman mumbles.

Mother laughs.

"*Shampoo*. Bought it at Fats'. There's none finer made, Herman. Do you know what it's made of? Soft soap, selenium, potash and borax! Have you ever heard of anything like it, Herman!"

"Rarely."

It smells almost like Mother does when she and Father go out on Saturday and come home late and have strange faces Sunday morning.

"Batten down the hatches!"

Mother turns on the shower and washes away the suds. Herman lets go of the cloth and sees the tube on the edge of the tub.

"Baby shampoo," he reads aloud, slowly. Baby shampoo.

Mother wraps his head in a towel.

"Everyone uses baby shampoo, Herman. Cliff Richard. Pat Boone. Elvis."

"Is that right? Kuppern too?"

"Of course. Can you manage from here, Herman?"

"One can manage."

When Mother has gone, Herman takes the chance. He unrolls the towel, rises to his toes in the bathtub and turns toward the mirror. There isn't much he can see, but it's more than enough. Most of his skull is completely visible now as if he has grown past his hair, through his hair. It can't be true, what Grandfather said about girls. Maybe it was in Tutankhamen's and the Hunchback of Notre Dame's time, before the *Flaskebekk* sank, but not now, in Herman's time. Herman slings the towel like a turban around his head again, runs to his room, turns off the light and the globe, collapses topsyturvy in the bed and fights with the comforter. And when it has gotten enough of a beating, he whales on the pillow and pajamas; it is Herman versus a smoke screen.

Later, Mother is sitting there. Herman lies on his stomach and holds his breath. He manages it for awhile. His eyes bulge like tomatoes. There are bass drums in his ears. Then he must give up. He pops the cork and shrivels together like an air mattress.

"Aren't you going to have supper?" Mother asks softly.

Herman doesn't answer.

"Dad's made a pile of sandwiches."

Herman still doesn't answer.

"Cucumber and salami and mayonnaise!"

Not a sound comes from Herman. Mother gives up and tries to find something else to say.

"You can stay up awhile, if you like. We can play cards."

"You just cheat."

"Do I cheat?"

"You cheat and lie."

"But we've talked about that, Herman. I didn't try to trick you. Of course I don't want to trick you."

"You said the wig was fine. It looks like a turd with a rubber band around it."

Mother is silent a long time thinking it over.

"Where did you put the wig, Herman?"

"Not saying."

"Have you thrown it away?"

"Rather not say."

Mother slips her hands into her lap and makes a knot of them.

"Soon you'll get a new wig, you know. And it's much nicer. It's made of real hair."

"I'm ugly," Herman whispers down in the pillow.

"What did you say?"

"I'm ugly! I'm ugly!"

"Don't say that, Herman. No one is ugly."

"Then I'm no one."

Mother lifts her hand, hesitates a little, then she puts it on Herman's head and strokes carefully through the thin wisps of hair that hang there. And then Herman remembers that she used to do that before, when he had lots of hair and it got too long, and he remembers that it was one of his favorite things, exactly that, when she stroked him through the hair, tugged it a little and laughed. Herman digs his face into the pillow. Mother leaves her hand on his head awhile longer, then she pulls it away, and it's so quiet that they can hear Father chewing bread out in the kitchen.

Then another sound comes. It comes from the bed, from the pillow.

"Are you crying, Herman?"

"Not at all."

"It's all right to cry."

"Got shampoo in my eyes."

"Does it sting?"

"A little."

"Then it's good to cry. It washes out your eyes."

"I'm not crying. Go!"

Mother gets up, opens the door, and the light from the hall paints the walls white.

"Goodnight!" Father calls.

"Goodnight," Mother whispers.

"G'night."

Then she closes the door finally. The room becomes black again, and Herman's eyes overflow. It's like being underwater, where everything is dark, silent and slow. He falls asleep down there, with his head against a jellyfish, and in a dream he ascends again, toward the surface, breaks through the thin, shiny membrane, rises slowly in the bed. And he sees that this world is just as dark and lonely.

Herman opens the closet where the costume hangs, puts on the long, black cape, the mask and the wide-brimmed hat, sticks the sword in the belt and is ready. He picks the door lock, listens, runs through the apartment, quick as the wind, silent as a bird. He slides down the banister to the first floor, sneaks into the back yard, climbs up the clothesline and hops over the fence like a puma, already fooling those who had thought to follow him.

Herman stands in the middle of Gabels Street and looks at the luminous ring around the full moon. It's a good sign. Then it's covered by black clouds, and the snow that falls right afterward hides his tracks.

He knows where he is going.

The sign at the Frogner Theater is turned off and the title has been taken down. Herman sneaks along the wall, and with the sword he breaks open the door where the public usually comes out.

He is inside!

He stops, listens again—no voices, no footsteps. Then he walks down the dark corridor with the weapon raised in case Monastario pops up. But he's surely sleeping now, after all the wine he has drunk. And the guards think they're safe.

That's where they're wrong.

Herman comes to a new door, presses the door handle down carefully and pushes it open with the sword. He looks into the auditorium. The curtain is drawn in front of the screen and a few bracket lamps light the wall like torches. Then Herman sees a man. He's sitting in the second row with his feet over the seat in front. He's dressed in a gray suit. He's reading a book.

Herman goes closer, and now he recognizes the man. It is Zorro, Zorro the way he usually is when he's not Zorro but the bookworm Don Diego.

Zorro is smart.

Herman sticks the sword in his belt, sits down next to him and puts his legs over the seat back too.

"What's the meaning of this?" Don Diego asks.

"Thought maybe you need a little help."

"Yes. With getting time to pass. The days are long waiting for the next episode. Soon I'll know this book by heart."

"What are you reading?"

"It's one I found here, fortunately. *Herman Wildenvey*.

"My name's Herman, too."

"Don Diego. I guess there's no danger in telling you that I also go by the name Zorro."

"I won't tell."

Don Diego sighs heavily.

"No, it was better when the Hunchback of Notre Dame visited here. I helped him in the end."

"Did it come out alright for the Hunchback and the lady?"

"Indeed, it went just fine. It usually docs, Herman. Even though he was out in bad weather."

They sit silently awhile and look at the checkered curtain hanging in front of the screen. Herman glances over at Don Diego now and then. He is much smaller than Herman thought. His face is pale and drawn as if he has been sitting inside too much lately reading difficult books. Herman starts to slightly regret putting on the secret costume.

"How's it going?" he asks quickly.

"Oh, as I said, time passes slowly and meaninglessly sometimes. Tornado is in the stall, and I must admit I'm a little bored with Bernardo's magic tricks. I've seen them many times before, you know, and he does the same ones over and over again. But Bernardo is a fine fellow. I couldn't manage without him."

"I meant the story, actually," Herman says. "How does it end?"

"I get out of the cell, then, you know. As I said, it usually comes out alright in the end. It's good to know. Otherwise I wouldn't have gone along with all of this."

"But how did you get out?"

"There's a loose stone in the floor. I wiggle it up with the sword and set it between the walls so that they stop before I get squeezed to death."

"That's pretty clever. And the young lady next to you?"

"I free her, of course, and guide her back to her real home after dramatic fencing battles."

Don Diego becomes thoughtful, and Herman doesn't want to disturb him.

"I think I am in love with her," says Don Diego finally. "And I don't quite know how that comes out. It bothers me, Herman."

"It's sure to go fine, Zorro. I mean Don Diego. It usually does."

"Nice way to put it, Herman."

Don Diego puts his hand on Herman's shoulder.

"Which of my stories do you like the best?"

Herman thinks it over.

"*The Black Horseman* and *The Mask Falls* are good. But *The Double* is the best."

"Yes, I could have guessed. But you don't go around in my outfit to shame me, do you?"

"No, and that's final," says Herman.

Don Diego sticks the book in his pocket and stands up. "It was nice talking to you, Herman. But now I must leave."

There is something Herman wants to say.

"Since you helped the Hunchback of Notre Dame, maybe you can help me too?"

Don Diego looks down at him and his face gets sad and thin in the glow from the bracket lamps.

"I cannot. You must manage yourself. Sorry, Herman."

"Sorry, Zorro."

Then Don Diego goes up on the stage, raises his hand in a final farewell and disappears behind the curtain.

17.

THE DAY THE CHRISTMAS street lights are lit, like shining cross- stitching through the entire city, Herman goes up to Jacobsen's Groceries. First he smells the coffee machine, but it isn't as good as before. He thinks it smells like rancid socks, and it doesn't really surprise him since everything else has also changed, and Herman isn't the same either. He pulls the cap down in front and stands at the counter. Jacobsen Jr. comes out from the back room, combs his hair backward in a high arch, sticks the comb in his breast pocket along with sixteen ball point pens, and leans toward Herman.

"Long time, no see. Where have you been lately?"

"Adapazari."

That's something Jacobsen Jr. will believe because the customer is always right.

"Was the weather nice there?"

"There was so much sun that we had to use an umbrella."

Jacobsen Jr. gets impatient and smiles crookedly like a movie star.

"And what will it be?"

"It will be two Christmas beers."

"Two Christmas beers, yes. Just two?"

"I have enough money."

"No doubt. And who are they for, if I might ask?"

He might. Herman lays the bills in front of Jacobsen Jr.

"For the Bottle Man."

"And you said *two* Christmas beers? *Two* Christmas beers for the Bottle Man. Don't make me laugh, Herman. What are you up to?"

"I'm not making you laugh."

And Jacobsen Jr. doesn't laugh either. He goes right out to the store room and fetches Mother. She inspects Herman and opens the flap in the counter.

"Aren't you in school today?"

"Took the day off."

"He claims he wants *two* Christmas beers for the Bottle Man," Jacobsen Jr. breaks in. "That would be the smallest order the Bottle Man has made since the war ended."

Mother looks at Herman again and her look intensifies.

"Is that true?"

"Honest to goodness!"

She comes closer and whispers in his ear.

"You aren't thinking about beering your hair again, I hope?"

"Never. I owe the Bottle Man two bottles."

Mother smiles and places a Christmas beer in each of his pockets.

"Hurry up now. The Bottle Man has surely had a hard winter."

Herman sprints around the corner, and even before he gets the door with Frantsén on it open, he hears many strange sounds. The Bottle Man is talking loudly to himself or Time, but it's impossible to understand what he's saying. He must be using his mother tongue. Now and then he screams and bottles break at even intervals. Herman waits a long time, but the noise doesn't end. So he goes in and sees the Bottle Man lying on the floor, digging wildly at the carpet with both hands.

"Are you looking for Time?" Herman asks.

But the Bottle Man doesn't hear. He continues to dig toward the wall, changes direction and creeps along the baseboard while he slings empty bottles aside.

"It couldn't have gone very far. Can I help?"

The Bottle Man rises suddenly and stares at Herman with

the biggest eyes he has ever seen. They look like dinner plates with old soufflé on them.

"Stop!" he yells. "Stop! Not another step!"

But Herman is standing on the threshold and hasn't even thought of moving for the time being.

"*Du våger inte träda i Kungens rosenbedd!*"

"I've got Christmas beer," Herman whispers.

The Bottle Man wipes the sweat off his forehead and stomps his foot.

"Can't you see I'm working!"

Suddenly he paces back and forth at full speed making sounds like a lawn mower.

"The Belgian royal house is expected! We must get everything ready. We must weed. We must sweep. We must rake. We must polish every single piece of gravel!"

He stops just as fast, shakes his hands in front of his face and takes a step closer to Herman.

"And we must get rid of all the animals! Do you hear! They pee and fool around. There's mice and snakes here! There's crabs and lobsters here! What do you think the Belgian royalty will think! The animals have to go! I've gotten rid of some. But not all! There's still a camel!"

The Bottle Man continues staring at Herman. Bits of food fall from his mouth, and he comes another step closer. His hair dangles down in front. His nostrils vibrate, and foam forms at the corners of his mouth.

"Have you set a world record now?" Herman asks quietly.

Then something happens with the Bottle Man. He begins to tremble. It starts at his hands, as if someone has lit a match in each finger. It snarls up through his arms and down both legs, and seems about to explode. But the Bottle Man doesn't go up in smoke. He just sinks down on the floor, quiet as a bag, and doesn't move.

Herman sets the bottles by the door and sneaks out backwards, and just then he sees it, the turtle. It's on its back next to the escritoire, among the empty bottles, with its stubby feet pointing in every direction and its green, wrinkled head sticking askew out of the shell.

The same evening, the ambulance comes and carries the Bottle Man away. Herman stands at the window of his room watching. The street is silent afterward.

Mother knocks on the door and he lets her in. She stops behind him, put her hands on his shoulders, and Herman holds the cap tightly.

"What are they doing with the Bottle Man?" he asks.

"They're going to dry him out awhile."

"On a clothesline?"

"Not exactly. He drank too much beer and got his head wet. Are you afraid, Herman?"

"The Bottle Man isn't dangerous."

Herman turns toward Mother.

"Are they going to bury his turtle now?"

"Sure they will."

"He probably just stepped on it."

"I think so too."

"He didn't see it, and then stepped on it. It's always dark at the Bottle Man's."

18.

HERMAN STAYS IN HIS ROOM. He sleeps with the light on. In the dark there are too many thoughts—even when the lamp in the ceiling is lit and the globe is shining, the thoughts come into his head like an ant trail through the ears and become a mound of questions. Is it true that time heals all wounds? Does time have a white coat and a nurse? Why can't time pull it's own tooth? How tall is the world's biggest dwarf? Why is the stomach satisfied quicker than the eyes? Does time come or go? Or does it just pass? Herman knows his hair is falling out. It happens every single night. In the morning he picks the hairs out of his cap and hides them in the herbarium in the bottom drawer. He opens the flaps in the Advent calendar and finds small animals he has no use for. Sometimes he wishes that he could creep into one of the openings and get lost in the forest behind the reindeer. Soon it smells of Christmas bread throughout the apartment, red stars come into view in all the windows and Advent candles burn down unevenly.

One day he has to go to school anyway. It's the Christmas exam. And now he's no longer invisible. Strange things happen. Now everyone suddenly wants to carry his school bag, give him the best sandwiches from their lunches, share sodas, hold the door for him and trade stamps, even though he doesn't collect stamps. Now they're feeling even more sorry for me, thinks Herman. Now they feel so sorry for me that they almost have to follow the Ten Commandments. He pretends the others are all invisible instead—that's the best. Only Ruby stands in the corner with her back to him. Herman decides not to see her either.

Barrel arrives and greets Herman first. Herman is busy filling the ink cartridge and looks the other way, but it's quite difficult not to see Barrel at all. Barrel is still growing. He fills the entire chalkboard across and has surely begun eating the Christmas ham already. He hits his desk hard with the pointer three times even though it has been quiet in the room for some time.

Then Barrel reads the story they must retell. All ears are tuned. Herman doesn't quite know whether he likes the story. But gradually, as Barrel reads, he becomes certain. He absolutely doesn't like it because it can't be true. Herman decides to make many mistakes and changes the ending.

Barrel puts down the book, sits behind the desk and closes one eye while the other looks around without blinking.

Herman writes:

Per and Kari go to the grocer for mother. They are going to buy flower, sugar butter and cheese. But on the way home there is a hole in the sugar bag. Kari holds the hole but the sugar pours out the hole way. Per and Kari were completely upset but mother said that it was not there falt. Fortunately there was a little sugar left in the bag. But Kari has to run back to the grocer again. There was a hole in the bag you see, said Kari. And so what, asked the grocer. There was a hole in the bag, repeats Kari and almost all the sugar ran out. You won't get a new bag of sugar from me, said the grocer. Then Kari got scared and ran away.

Afterward is arithmetic. Herman takes away instead of adds. Then he turns in the papers before the bell rings and wanders out of the classroom with all the silent eyes on his back. But Barrel doesn't come after him. Now they are so sorry for me that I can do whatever I want, thinks Herman.

He might as well walk down to the city.

There are skiers in the streets. Eight streetcars are derailed at Riddervolds Square and the snow banks are at least three meters high. The store windows are full of short elves who look angry, and where Welhaven once sat on his pedestal, long bored with himself, sits the Abominable Snowman with a bunch of dirty pigeons on top. When they make a statue of me, Herman thinks, when they make a statue of me, I'll ask Vigeland to make a huge bronze pigeon on my head too.

But on Karl Johan, the Christmas tree is ready, like a green Sputnik. On the ground lie big gifts in weathered paper, and most of them look soft. It's the gifts for the poor who can't afford their own Christmas trees to put gifts under. Herman gets an idea. He takes the wig out of his school bag, rolls it in wax paper from his lunch, rushes across the street, greets the lady from the Salvation Army, and puts his gift with the others.

The Salvation lady, who has a black box on her head and round glasses that fog up over red cheeks, bends her knees and talks to Herman.

"That's a good boy. Who thinks of others!"

"One follows the Ten Commandments. Merry Christmas."

Then Herman goes to Studenten. Old ladies and men stand there sipping cocoa with pointy mouths and big noses. He goes to the counter, and a waiter with a white pencil-box-shaped cap on the top of his head comes into sight above the cash register.

"A chocolate milkshake, a strawberry milkshake, an ice cream float and a banana split with lots of almonds. My mother will pay."

Herman carries the goods over to the shelf by the window, thinks it over, and begins in the middle. He has to loosen his belt buckle two notches while he's at it, but as he's about to eat the banana, the waiter stands next to him, pushing the pencil box backward and scratching at his hairline.

"Where's your mother?" he asks.

"At Jacobsen's Groceries."

"Where did you say?"

"I said Jacobsen's Groceries in Skillebekk. She works there."

What happens now happens fast. The man tears the banana from Herman and he is hauled into a room behind the counter. He's pressed down in a chair while the waiter gets the telephone book. In the corner, a huge box is shaking. It looks like a washing machine. That must be where they make the icecream soft, Herman thinks and comes up with something. From cows we also get milkshakes and banana splits.

"What's your name?" shouts the waiter, even though he's just three inches away.

"I'm not hard of hearing," says Herman.

But the waiter shouts all the louder. Maybe he has eaten too many bananas.

"My name is Herman Fulkt. You can't do anything to me."

"What did you say we can't?"

"They feel sorry for me."

"Yes, I can promise you that!"

"You promise?"

The waiter barely manages to hit the right numbers on the dial. He shouts in the telephone too and slings the receiver down like a hammer thrower.

"Can I get a soft ice cream while I wait?" Herman asks.

Then the waiter cracks. He cracks like a lemming in Valdres. The buttons on the white coat fly in all directions, the cap falls off his head, and his tie goes straight in the air.

"Hold your mouth, you troublemaker!"

"I'm full anyway," says Herman.

"And take off your cap when you talk to grown-ups!"

"You said I should hold my mouth."

"Are you being impudent too!"

"I'm not talking to grown-ups anymore today."

"Take off your cap!"

"No."

"Didn't you hear me!"

"No, and that's final!"

The waiter grabs the edge of the cap. Herman holds it. He holds it with all his powers, but there aren't many of them. The waiter tears off the cap, stumbles backwards, suddenly gets a surprised expression on his mouth and his entire face freezes. He stares at Herman, at Herman's head, at Herman's skull, and his eyes begin to waver, as if they belong somewhere else, and slowly he holds out the cap.

"Here," says Herman.

The waiter lets it drop in his lap, and Herman twists it on.

"Do you. . .do you still want a soft ice cream?"

Herman understands everything then.

A half hour later Mother comes, pays the bill without a word, grabs Herman by the arm and pulls him up Karl Johan.

"This wasn't any fun, Herman!"

"It was pretty good."

"You could have asked for money, couldn't you!"

"That would have been wise."

"We could even have gone together!"

Herman feels something down in his stomach, almost like the time he swallowed a leaf, but this feels heavier and more dangerous.

"I think I have to go to the bathroom," he says.

"Do you think or do you know!"

"I think I know."

"How much did you eat?"

"Three-and-a-half. Think we should hurry."

Herman feels it coming.

"I know we should hurry."

They run up Dramens Road and get there just in time. Herman races to the bathroom in a new personal record, and it's one of the best feelings he has had in a long time. But it's a little sad too, that so much good is gone so quickly. Now the eels will get fat, thinks Herman.

Then he hears Father take a triple jump up the stairs, and he sounds rather excited.

"Herman! Where's Herman!"

"In the bathroom," Mother says.

Father stands outside the door and almost can't manage to speak clearly.

"Herman! You know what!"

"Don't know."

"Zorro's here!"

Herman is silent.

"Are you in there?" Father shouts.

"Yes. Is Zorro here?"

"Zorro's back at Frogner! I've got tickets for the five o'clock show. Hurry up!"

"I've had a busy day."

"What's that, Herman?"

And he really doesn't want to, but feels he has to go so that Father can see the next episode. So much happens inside him at the same time that it almost makes his head hurt.

He flushes so Father can't hear if he suddenly has to cry.

"Coming," Herman says.

Then they're sitting in the theater again, in the second row. The bracket lamps slowly die out, and it crackles behind the screen as the curtain goes to the sides. The silence falls and becomes a hissing syllable that ravages lowly through the audience. But something is wrong. There's something that doesn't fit. Zorro is suddenly on a mountain top along with the lady, and that's not the way it ended last time. There's a loud uproar. Everyone gets up at the same time, and in the opening up by the ceiling they can see the projectionist's horror stricken face. Herman recognizes him. He was the one who glued up the titles and later was the doorman.

"Remain seated!" he shouts. "Or we'll have to cancel the show! There's chocolate for sale at the snack bar!"

The lights come up, the curtain is pulled closed and everything starts over. Finally there's a flash over the screen. The projectionist has found the right reel, and Zorro is in the cell as the walls get closer and closer from both sides. Everyone leans forward, holds their breath, holds each other, everyone except for Herman.

He pokes Father in the shoulder.

"There's surely a loose stone in the floor that he can get up," Herman whispers.

And in the end Zorro rides Tornado toward the horizon. He turns and watches the pretty lady, who is somewhere else entirely. And Herman can see that behind the black mask are sad eyes, sad because she didn't come with him, or because he didn't remain.

As they walk home, there's a full moon in the sky that

lights up their faces as if they're wearing white disguises. Then a black cloud comes over the city, and only the stars in the windows are visible.

"By god, you're sharp, Herman!"

"Just guessed."

"Boy, I never would have thought of that. I thought Bernardo would conjure him out."

Father laughs, stops Herman and takes out a cigarette butt.

"You haven't seen this. Watch!"

He hides the cigarette in his hand, clenches the other fist also, and does a bunch of motions with his arms as if he's trying to get rid of a fly. It goes by quite fast. Then he reaches out his hands.

"Which hand is it in?"

Herman points to the left fist.

Father opens it, nothing there.

"Try again!"

Herman points at the right fist.

Father opens it too. The cigarette isn't there either.

But then he opens his mouth instead, works with his tongue awhile, and suddenly the butt comes out. It hangs over his lip, and Father appears astonished himself too.

"Gee," he says.

"Geez-es," says Herman.

They walk on and search for openings in the snow bank. They find one at Solli Square.

"What do you want the very most for Christmas?" Father says.

Herman doesn't answer that.

"Shouldn't I have said that?"

"Yes. What do you want, Dad?"

"A surprise."

"Same here."

Herman makes a snowball, throws it at a lamppost and misses. Father tries it too and doesn't hit either. They walk a ways without saying anything. From an open window comes the sound of a Christmas song and an out-of-tune piano.

"Is Grandfather coming for Christmas Eve?" Herman asks.

"I suppose so. We can get him that evening. The two of us can carry him down the stairs, don't you think?"

"It'll be really nice."

When they get home there's a huge spruce in the hall. It looks very fresh. There's still snow on the branches and shiny marks from the axe. Mother is there too with her arms crossed.

"Bock and Rags were here," she says. "With the Christmas tree."

Father measures it, plucks at the needles, and is very keen.

"I see. Fine tree. Very fine tree. With some decorations here and there and a star."

"Did they buy it at Frogner Church or the Vestkant market, do you think?" Mother asks.

"Well, I don't know. It doesn't really matter."

"They said it was free," Mother continues. "Absolutely free."

"We lucked out there," Father says, beginning to get restless.

"Free!" Mother declares for the third time. "And how can that be?"

Now Father has changed facial colors and doesn't look like he's having a very good time at all.

"Oh yeah, now I remember! Rags' brother-in-law has a piece of forest at Hadeland!"

Mother examines Father up and down and doesn't say a word. Herman knows that something isn't as it should be. He starts feeling sorry for Father.

"Those who call in the forest will get an answer," Herman says and hurries into this room.

He doesn't get to sleep. Everything has become so resonant. He can hear his heart beat deep inside his ear. He can hear the hair fall from his head. It is so resonant that he can hear the clock all the way over at Grandfather's strike ten. And he can hear his parents' voices in the living room even though the radio is on too loud with a program he doesn't like.

"I think it's disgraceful," Mother says.

"Since when are you so prudish!" Father shouts, stomps out to the kitchen, opens the pantry and unscrews a cap.

"Don't scream like that," Mother says. "Herman can hear you."

"Herman's asleep."

"Yes. And you'll wake him with that whining."

"Who's whining now, huh!"

But Herman isn't sleeping, and they cannot wake him. He listens, but he doesn't want to hear. He lies completely still so he won't be caught red-handed. And all the other sounds are gone now. Only his parents' voices are there, loud and painful. Don't talk anymore, Herman thinks. They must not say any more. Trim the Christmas tree. Trim the Christmas tree. Don't talk to each other anymore.

"Brother-in-law at Hadeland! That's a good one, Dad. Now why don't you tell me where that spruce came from."

"Bock and Rags said they could get some cheap trees. And so I took them up on it!"

"Where?" Mother asks.

Awhile passes before Father answers.

"Are you going to get drunk right before Christmas now? Hmm!"

Now Mother has gotten as tough as Grandmother was when Grandfather wanted to drink beer, Herman thinks. And now they stop talking. They've become mute. They've become mute on the spot.

"Nordmarka," Father says at long last. "Behind Sognsvann."

"Grown men! You ought to be ashamed!"

"Do you know how much a tree like this costs this year! No! And how much that new wig costs? A thousand crowns. At least!"

Herman turns off the light, closes his eyes and hides under the comforter. But it doesn't help. There is nowhere to hide where no one can find him. He bites his teeth together and sings inside in order not to hear any more. *Now the bells peal, ring and summon, ring and summon from a thousand towers.* Ready or not, here I come. *The tune of salvation, call and welcome, call and welcome God's children with peace.*

And Herman falls asleep, cap first.

He is awakened by a finger. The finger is one of five. It

becomes a hand. The hand hangs on an arm that belongs to Mother.

"You sleepyhead," she says. "It's almost eleven."

"I was under cover," Herman says, sitting up in bed.

"Aren't you going to church with your class today?" Mother asks.

Herman turns away.

"The minister probably won't let me keep my cap on."

"He'll say the same things as last year anyway."

"'And if any of you find Him in the manger like the shepherds saw, then you possess enough to boldly die and yet live on.'"

Herman has to lie down just from exhaustion. Mother is impressed.

"You could do all that from memory, Herman?"

"It's in the Advent calendar," he mumbles. "What's a manger?"

"That's where Jesus lay when he was born."

"It must have been bad."

"Shall we open it together, Herman."

"You do it."

She folds out a flap and finds one of the kings in red plastic. He has a hole in his head.

"I'd better hurry, Herman. Or Junior will get angry."

She begins to laugh deep in her stomach and up to her mouth.

"Do you know what a customer asked him yesterday? 'Do you have pig's feet, Jacobsen Jr.?' "

"Heard that last year," says Herman.

"Of course."

"But it is quite funny."

A siren sounds far away. Maybe it's the Bottle Man, Herman thinks. Maybe they're still driving him around in the ambulance at full speed in order to dry out his head?

"Then I'll be off," Mother says.

Herman raises himself in bed.

"Are you broke, Mother?"

Her jaw drops and it looks strange, but then she starts

laughing at the same time as she lifts it back in place.

"I'm dumb, Herman."

"Yes."

"I had completely forgotten. There's so much to do before Christmas, you know."

"One is very busy."

She finds two orange bills in her purse and lays them next to the king on the pillow.

"That wasn't what I meant."

But Herman doesn't know how to get it said. He can't shout out that he listened and heard what they were saying the night before, and he can't say what he really wants to say.

"What was it you meant then, Herman?"

It burns behind his eyes, but there's no shampoo nearby to blame it on. He turns toward the wall and stares at the calendar with all the open flaps in the middle of the forest with reindeer.

"Whether you went broke at Studenten," he whispers.

Mother pats him on the back.

"I promised you a trip there," she says. "If I'd gone along, we'd surely have eaten twice as much."

Afterward, when he is alone again, he takes Mother's shopping bag cart and goes up to Jansen's Short Goods on Drammens Road. The lady behind the counter is also rather short, with a face that barely reaches over the counter.

"What do you have?" Herman asks.

"Ask what we don't have instead," says Mrs. Jansen, standing on a stool for height.

"So you have that too?"

Herman looks around. There are shelves with hardwares on all the walls, pencils, teaspoons, thimbles, matches and tweezers. This must be where dwarfs go when they need something, he thinks.

"But do you have tall goods too?" Herman asks.

"We keep those in the back room," Mrs. Jansen says, hopping down from the stool.

"Then I guess I'll take two tall and one quite short."

Then he rolls home, closes the door and puts the gifts as

far as they'll go under his bed. There's two crowns and seventy-eight øre change. Herman wonders what he'll use it for and decides to save it in the bottom shelf in case Father doesn't have enough for bread and butter some day.

He takes out the herbarium and looks through the collection. There soon won't be room for any more hair. I had this much, Herman thinks. This much is left. It's not much. The cap itches on his skull and it's beginning to get too big. It glides down over his eyes all the time. He takes a peek at the club hair. It doesn't look so dangerous.

In the evening, Mother and Father trim the tree. Mother balances on a stool and hangs up Christmas baskets and fake cones. Father tries to fasten the star, but it looks quite crooked. They turn toward Herman together as he stands on the threshold and doesn't quite know if he is on the way out or the way in.

"Hi, Herman. Are you coming to help us?"

"You'll manage by yourselves," Herman says.

19.

NOT UNTIL HERAMN OPENS flap number 24 and finds
Jesus does he remember that it's Christmas Eve. It's like any
other day. Father is at the construction site lifting the roof
in place, and Mother is at the grocery store selling rib roasts
that look like stall bars. Only Easter morning extinguishes
sorrow. He must wait all the way until the evening, and he's
not certain whether he's looking forward to it either.

He takes a peek under the bed; the gifts are still there.
Then he stands by the window. The sky is overflowing with
sun, but the trees on the other side of the street aren't green
and glittering. They have thick, white branches that are on
the point of breaking. And no one says good day to them either. The people outside walk quickly and have more than
enough to carry. A bell peals and someone is already singing Christmas carols. Can one eat the peel of a bell? Herman thinks. Can the fellowship sail on the Indian Ocean? And
is Grandfather just as bored passing the time in his canopy
bed?

He decides he may as well visit Grandfather and give him
his gift. He hurries through the slushy streets, past the per-
fumery where all the men stand at the counter buying 4711,
past the post office where the last Christmas cards are being
sent and arrive too late to cousins in the country, past the
Christmas trees standing in bunches that are so ugly no one

will buy them so they get turned into wrapping paper instead, past the doors where wreaths and spruce sprigs hang with cones and raisins in them.

Nothing hangs on Grandfather's door, but it is open. Herman goes in, hiding the gift behind his back, and sneaks over to the canopy bed. Grandfather is sleeping and he hasn't let go of the photograph of Grandmother. Herman doesn't quite know whether he should wake him. It looks like he's sleeping well. His face is still as water. It's the stillest he has ever seen.

Then he hears something else. The clock in the corner has stopped.

"Grandfather," Herman says.

Nothing happens in the canopy bed.

"Grandfather? Herman here. Are you there?"

He waits, but no answer comes.

"I have my Christmas present for you. It's not so very fine, but I bought it myself."

Herman tries talking loudly. It doesn't help either. He sits on the chair and carefully puts his hand on Grandfather's head.

"Are you fooling me?"

Grandfather doesn't notice. His face is soft and almost white. Herman pulls back his hand quickly.

"Are you sure you're not fooling?"

He still gets no answer. He pushes the chair closer to the bed.

"Have I told you about the person who lost his hair?" Herman begins. "Someone I knew. From class. It fell out little by little even though there was no war. It fell out on its own. Are you listening, Grandfather? That's good. And so he hid the hair in his herbarium so he wouldn't lose it altogether. Do you think that was smart, Grandfather? See, he thought that one fine day or another he'd have use for it. His parents couldn't afford a real wig for him, you see. But the finest hair he had was club hair. If anyone teased him, he would just club them right down with it. Don't you think that's smart, Grandfather? But did he have to hit so hard? Maybe he just needed to show his club hair, and then everyone would leave him alone. How did it come out for him? Don't really know. He probably went around with a cap on the rest of his life and didn't get much out of it. Nonsense, you say? No it isn't, Grandfather."

Herman takes off his cap and shows his head. A few tufts of hair hang where the part once was.

"You knew all the time, didn't you, Grandfather? But you just didn't say anything?"

Grandfather doesn't say anything now either.

"You're not fooling me," whispers Herman.

He rises and has almost forgotten why he came. He lays the gift on the chair and thinks.

"Maybe I'll unwrap it for you? I think I'll do that."

He rips off the paper and opens the box.

"If they don't fit, it doesn't matter if you exchange them."

He puts on his cap and looks at Grandfather's hands awhile, still holding the photograph of Grandmother.

"You have laces, don't you, Grandfather?"

Then Herman sets a pair of shiny, black shoes next to the bed and walks slowly homeward.

Herman takes hold of the trunk with both hands and shakes all he can. He shakes until the Christmas baskets and cones fall off. He shakes until the elves lose their foothold and the lights fall down. He shakes until the star falls like a shot, and he shakes until the needles loosen and fly through the room. Then he sits on the floor, under the naked, gray branches, and he looks like a gift that no one has bothered to wrap and that isn't to anyone.

After a long while he hears his parents come home. They call to him. He doesn't answer. Right away they are standing at the door. They remain there a long time, looking at him and gaping in silence.

Herman huddles up at the base of the Christmas tree and covers his eyes. They see him anyway. Mother takes a step into the room. At first she speaks very softly, then her voice grows in both strength and speed.

"Herman? Herman! What have you done now! Did you destroy the Christmas tree! Herman!"

Father tears himself free from the door jam, storms across the floor, hoists Herman up by both arms and holds him there.

"Have you gone completely mad, boy!"

Mother runs from one wall to the other.

"I'm really getting tired of this now!" she shouts. "You can't do this! Speak to me, Herman!"

"Grandfather is dead."

Mother suddenly stops. Father slowly sets him down and lets go.

"What did you say, Herman?"

"Grandfather is dead."

Mother comes toward him and almost doesn't have a voice left in her mouth.

"Have you been with Grandfather today, Herman?"

"Grandfather is dead. Are we going to have a yule log now?"

Mother heads out into the hall. Father follows but stops and turns to Herman.

"I'll stay here," says Herman. "Said 'bye to Grandfather."

Then they run off. Herman hears their rapid footsteps disappear down the stairs. He stands in the middle of the living room and waits until everything is as quiet as possible. Then he tries to straighten up after himself. He hangs the decorations on the tree again, climbs up on the table and fastens the star, but can't get the needles on. They won't stick. They've fallen off for good. He gets a broom instead, sweeps them together in a pile and puts them in the waste pail. He takes it with him, but on the way out he stops at his room. He hesitates even though deep inside he has made up his mind. But it takes a longer time for the feet and hands to be sure of their cause. Finally they reach agreement; he hurries in, takes out the herbarium and empties all the hair in the pail too.

Then he goes down in the back yard and throws everything in the trash can there.

Herman's parents don't come home until the Silver Boys

sing Christmas songs on the radio on the floor above. Mother has streaks on her face, almost like a window that has been rained on. Father holds her and they sit down in the living room.

"Where is Grandfather now?" Herman asks.

"He's in a room at the hospital," Father says softly.

"Is that where time heals all wounds?"

Mother blows her nose a long time and stands up.

"Let's open presents!" she suddenly says.

"Do you think we should?" Father says. "Surely we can wait till tomorrow. Right, Herman?"

"Sure."

"Grandfather will be angry if we don't open the presents today!"

Herman is restless.

"Can Grandfather be angry when he's dead?"

"He would have been angry if he lived," Mother says.

"Then it's probably best if we open them right away."

Then they get the gifts under each of their beds and put them at the base of the Christmas tree.

"To Herman from Mother and Father!" Father reads on a tag and gives him the largest package.

Herman slowly takes off the paper and has a stomach-ache. He finds a box first, lifts the lid and only gets out two words, but it takes him quite a long time to say them.

"Spe-e-e-ed skates!"

He has to try them on right away. They're a little big, and he totters around the room on the leather.

"You have to have room to grow, you know," Mother says. "With extra socks and some newspaper they'll be fine."

"Thanks."

"There'll be a Norwegian record soon now," Father says, putting an arm on his back, showing a Chinese start. But before he takes the first stroke, he straightens up and bends his head toward Mother.

"I'm sorry. Shouldn't be carrying on like that today."

"Nonsense!" Mother says and picks out a new package. "From Herman to Father!"

"To me!" he shouts and tugs off the paper.

He is quiet a rather long time. Then the ability to speak returns.

"Three balls of yarn. Red, white and blue. That's not so bad."

Herman is a little confused and totters to the Christmas tree.

"I guess I mixed up the tags," he whispers. "That one's for Mother."

Father exhales in relief and turns the yarn over to Mother.

"Thank you very much, Herman. What would you like me to knit for you?"

"How about a speed skating suit?"

"Then you'd better make it real big, Mom," Father laughs, "since it won't be finished for years."

"Oh, hold your mouth, you!"

"I just meant that Herman is going to grow like crazy."

He picks out another package with his long arms.

"From Herman to Mother. This one's for me, then?"

"It looks that way."

Father carefully unwraps it and looks slyly at Herman.

"Two hundred meters of line! Wow, thanks a lot! Now those eels will get caught!"

"That's what I was thinking."

"Here's another gift, look!" Mother says. "From Grandfather to Herman!"

"From Grandfather?"

"That's what the tag says. From Grandfather to Herman."

"How could he walk?"

"He probably got some help."

"Well, that's good."

He feels the package first. It is soft and quite small. Then he opens it without destroying the paper and has to sit down.

"A skating cap," he whispers. "A skating cap."

He twists off the old cap and gets the new one on quickly. It fits like a glove, with three stripes and a point at the front. He gets to his feet and balances around the room with his head horizontal.

"Thanks, Grandfather," he shouts. "Thank you, too, very much!"

Mother looks at Father, and Father has something behind his back.

"By thunder, here's another package," he says. "From Mother and Father to Herman!"

It gets so quiet as he's opening it that he gets a stomach-ache again. He folds the paper aside. It is a box with foreign words on it.

"Heartfelt thanks. I can use it to keep my chestnuts in."

They come closer around him.

"You have to open the box too," Mother says.

"If you say so."

There's a knot inside him that gets tighter and tighter. He opens the box as slowly as he can and sees what's in it.

"It's a wig," Herman says.

"And it's rcal human hair," Father explains.

"Whose?"

"No, whose? It's yours now."

"You didn't steal it?"

Father turns to Mother and fumbles with two hundred meters of line.

"You know we didn't," she says. "It's hair from people who already have too much."

"From Hadeland?"

Now Herman's parents look at each other a long time, and Father has already made a tangle. Mother breathes heavily through her nose and sits down next to Herman.

"Look, it's exactly the same color as your hair! And the part is on the right side. Can even wash it in shampoo. Won't you try it on."

"Sure."

His fingers are completely stiff and don't want to co-operate.

"Turn around."

They look away. Herman takes off the skating cap and puts the wig on. It's softer that the last one, has bangs, and it's just as if his head is lighter, as if it isn't his any longer, but a head he has gotten from abroad.

"Can we look now?"

"Sure."

They look and talk at the same time.

"It's marvelous, Herman!" Mother says.

"I've never seen anything better," Father says.

They want to feel it. Herman twists himself away.

"You said that last time too."

"Let's go look in the mirror, okay?"

"No, and that's final."

"You look exactly like before!"

Father bites his tongue and can't talk anymore that Christmas Eve.

"Turn around!"

They do as Herman says. He lifts off the wig, lays it back in the box and puts on the skating cap again.

"Olly, olly, oxen free. Think I'll go to bed."

They follow him to his room. Herman hides the box with the wig in the bottom drawer.

"Shouldn't we have a little to eat?" Mother asks.

"I've seen so much today. I'm satisfied."

"But don't you think it's best if you take off the skating cap?"

"The last pair skates alone," says Herman.

And so he falls asleep, in the turn, with one arm free, and on the straightaway is Grandfather with a scheme to set the world's record.

20.

THERE'S A NEW FILM at Frogner. Zorro has gone home to Mexico, but Herman isn't going to the theater. He's going to the doctor again. Mother takes his hand and accompanies him to the waiting room. There's a line there and only one empty chair. And the people waiting are sicker than ever. They've unbuttoned their trousers and there is a row of buckets on the floor. They hold their hands to their mouths, complaining through their fingers, while they sway back and forth and shut their eyes until their faces resemble red apples. It doesn't smell good in there even though the window is open and it's below zero. It smells like the sewer at Fred Olsen Wharf plus old slippers with pork rinds in them.

"Happy New Year," Herman says.

He certainly shouldn't have said that. It starts sputtering and thundering in every direction as if their pockets are full of fireworks and burning matches. They surely have eyes that are satisfied before their stomachs, Herman thinks, pulling the skating cap down over his nose.

The doctor barely sticks his head out the door and motions them in with his index finger. He slams the door shut after himself, runs over to his place and lights a cigar.

"It's like this every year. Rib bones caught crosswise, food down the wrong pipe, cooked cabbage that won't come out. And as usual I forgot my gas mask. Does the cigar bother you, Herman?"

"Not at all."

"You haven't overeaten, have you?"

"We barely have bread and butter."

Mother gets up and walks twice around the chair.

"Well, well," says the doctor. "Did you get much for Christmas?"

The doctor is in such a good mood that Herman is suspicious.

"Are you going to use the needle now?"

"No, no. No needles at all. Cross my heart."

"A skating cap."

Then Herman sees that there's a different nurse there. And the doctor doesn't have a cold any longer. And on the windowsill is a new plant with red shoots that aim at the ceiling.

"Did you also get nice things for Christmas?" he asks.

The doctor answers with a cloud of smoke and a minute of silence.

"Let's take a peek again," he finally says, laying down the cigar and coming over to Herman.

"There certainly isn't much to look at."

"I'll do it anyway. If you take off the skating cap I won't have to use glasses."

Herman looks at the new nurse.

"Does she have to see too?"

"I'll turn around," she says quickly, turns her back and waters the plant.

"She's pretty agreeable," says Herman. "What's her name?"

Then he pulls the skating cap off and the doctor looks in his magnifying glass and pinches all over Herman's skull. He doesn't say a word while he does this, and Herman was right. There isn't much to look at. There are only two tufts of hair at the neck to speak of, and they aren't much to brag about either. The doctor is finished after one round, sticks the magnifying glass in his pocket and sits down again.

"You can put on your skating cap now, Herman."

It's already in place. The nurse has finished watering the

plant. The red shoots have become flowers in the meantime.

"What distance do you like the best?" the doctor asks.

"The four hundred meters. I'll be in a championship."

"He's joined the Oslo Skating Club," Mother says, walking toward the doctor. "There isn't anything to keep him from doing athletics?"

"No, no, not at all. Let him keep up with it."

"How. . . how does it look?"

The doctor looks with one eye on Mother, one on Herman, and one on the nurse.

"As I said, there isn't much to say. It went as we expected. And it must run it's course. The hair can come back. Or it might not come back."

He bends over the table toward Herman.

"Do you have pain anywhere?"

Herman feels around.

"Not that one knows of."

"Fine. And otherwise you feel good?"

"I'm healthy as a fish."

When he has said that, he gets the urge to bite his tongue, as Father does now and then. And he gets pains a few places anyway, in the stomach and eyes. He has not forgotten that Grandfather is dead and buried.

"Not exactly like a fish," he says lowly. "But maybe like a sock."

The doctor looks at Mother.

"Haven't you considered getting a wig?"

"We've done it. But he doesn't want to use it."

The doctor gets up, and Herman does the same."

"You don't want to use it? Why in all the world not?"

Herman looks down.

"Speed skaters don't wear wigs."

21.

HERMAN SITS BY THE TURN at Frogner Stadium and tightens his laces. He has two thick extra socks and the morning edition of *Aftenposten* in each skate. On the infield spin girls in short dresses casting shadows to every direction in the floodlights. Herman pulls on his mittens, pushes off, and glides on the ice. It goes well. It's ten minutes until the start.

He takes a few strokes with his arm free. The skating suit is tight around his knees and the newspaper rustles. But at least he isn't stepping on the inside leather. Music suddenly comes from the loudspeakers, Hammond organ and trumpet, and the girls on the infield make figure eights instead with one leg in the air. Herman can't see Ruby among them.

He begins to brake in the middle of the homestretch side, but doesn't stop before the start of the next curve. He supports himself on the snow bank on the way back, pretending he temporarily seriously injured his right knee, and places himself with the other speed skaters. He doesn't know any of them. So they don't know him. Everyone measures each other with indifferent looks. Herman is the only one with a genuine speed skating cap.

The starter comes down from the platform. He has the world's biggest thighs, and his rear sticks out like a camel's hump. But he doesn't have a pistol. He only has a whistle around his neck and a stopwatch. He is surely Egg's cousin.

He starts calling out the pairings. Two-by-two they get ready. Herman is to go last. He's going alone.

The starter glides over to him.

"Someone must go alone, you know. One of the racers hasn't come. Can't divide nine by two."

"Four and a half."

"Right. But first and foremost we race against ourselves. Remember that."

"Then it's good that I'm not very good," Herman says.

The starter backs up to the starting line. The first pair is ready, with bent backs and quivering legs, like two bumble-bees who have caught sight of a fly swatter. Then they break out, scrape around the turn, chase each other on the straight-away and finish in one piece at 53.8 and 56.4. The second pair bungles the lane change and begins a huge fist fight that lasts all the way to the last turn. There, the inner pulls away and storms over the finish at 1:04.5, while the outer glides in backwards at 1:12.7. But when the third pair is on the home stretch, and Herman is hoping one of them will fall, he hears two skates come to a quick stop behind him.

"What's with the newspaper, Herman?"

He turns slowly. It's Ruby. She looks down at his skates, where *Aftenposten* is sticking up from the leather. He looks at her feet. She has speed skates on. Ruby has on speed skates and a blue speed skating suit.

"Are you going to figure skate in those?" Herman whispers.

"I'm in the 400 meters," Ruby says.

She doesn't say anything more. She just glides over to the starter in one stroke. And Herman knows it's too late. It's too late to turn. He can't pull out now. He has to go to the start-ing line. He has to race against Ruby. He should never have wished for the third pair to fall.

Then he's standing ready in the inner lane, bending his knees and stretching his arms out to the side. The music from the loudspeakers stops, and all the figure skating girls who can't be more than eight wave to Ruby. Herman peeks over at her under his arm. She has her head almost down on the ice and her hands on her back. She must not cross in front of me, Herman thinks. She must not change first from the outer lane. She must not beat me. Then I may as well sell my skates and go to Adapazari and live in a cave the rest of my sorry days.

The starter blows in the whistle and Herman stumbles out. He hears Ruby's skates hit the ice. He sees that she is leaving him behind. He sees that she is pulling away. He leans into the turn, but doesn't get his legs shuffled, doesn't get one knee over the other. He can't hold the edge of snow and swerves into the outer lane. Ruby is already on the straightaway with both arms free. She has already changed by the time Herman crawls out of the turn. He gets his skates free of each other, crouches down and strides forward. But Ruby just increases her lead, and he can hear the shouts from the infield, and he knows he has lost. What if I fall in the last turn, he thinks. If I fall in the last turn before Ruby reaches the finish, then I can say I would have beaten her if I had stayed up. What if I break my leg? What if a German Shepherd comes out on the track and bites off my arm? What if the ice suddenly melts?

He has a lot of time to think on the back straightaway. But he doesn't fall. He manages not to fall. He stands upright through the turn and guides the way with his hand, and when he gets to the home stretch, Ruby has long since finished. Herman takes three desperate strokes, glides past the starter who calls 1:28.5. He hears laughter in the floodlights and continues right into the locker room.

Ruby catches up with him at the Oscar Mathisen statue. She has tied her skates together, and they are hanging over her shoulder. Herman has his in a bag on his back. Herman wants to keep going, but she gets in front of him.

"Didn't know you speed skated too," says Ruby.

Herman says nothing and wants to get past her.

"Have you trained much?"

"Forty days and forty nights."

"Why aren't you in school?"

"I'm contagious."

"Barrel said that we'll be expelled if we're not nice to you."

"I know. To hell with the whole mess."
Ruby looks at him more closely.
"Are you mad?"
"One is injured."
"Where?"
"I think it's in the knee."
Then he changes lanes in front of her and takes many detours home. When he gets there, he hangs the bag in the cellar and puts the skating cap in the bottom drawer.

22.

THE DAYS ARE COLD AS a refrigerator and just as dark inside. Only now and then does the door open, Mother and Father want to get a hold of him, but they can't. No one's going to get a hold of Herman. He sits deep inside with the globe in his lap, and they do not have arms long enough.

But one evening, when Mother is at a parent's meeting at school and Father is working overtime, Herman puts on the old cap without the tassel, puts the chestnuts in his pocket and goes out.

The streets are deserted. The sky is a black blanket drawn over the city, and the moon is a yellow tear. A wind from the north makes the snow swirl up under the streetlights, and everywhere are old Christmas trees, looking like skeletons or rusty bicycle wrecks.

Herman eels along the walls of buildings, listens, hears only the wind and snow and his own breath, white and cold. He sees an open window on Balders Street, is going to throw a chestnut in that direction, changes his mind, and runs all he can as if he did it anyway. He climbs up Bonde Hill and slinks over to Urra School. There are lights in some of the windows where the parents are meeting and drinking coffee. He sneaks around the corner and peeks into the schoolyard—it is abandoned, and all the footprints are covered over with snow.

Then he hears voices from up in the park. He goes there and sees Glenn, Karsten and Bjørnar. They're standing in a tight circle by the fence and are up to something.

Herman hurries over to them.

They immediately stop talking and stare at him.

"What're you doin' here?" Glenn asks.

"Passing through."

They start to laugh between themselves, and Karsten pulls him nearer.

"Which place did you take in speed skating?"

Herman clenches his teeth, turns toward the church and follows the spire with his eyes until it disappears like a copper needle in the pull of the sky.

"What are you doing?" Herman asks.

"Nothing you'd dare, you sissy," says Bjørnar.

Herman takes a chestnut out of his pocket and throws it at the school. Right afterward they hear the powerful splintering of glass.

"I must have hit it," whispers Herman.

"You hit the principal's office!" they shout.

They all run away and don't stop until they get to the statue of Welhaven. They hide behind him, and then Glenn pulls out a green clothesline.

"What are you going to do with that?" Herman asks.

"Hang you out to dry."

"I'm not wet in the head."

Glenn makes a noose in one end.

"Tie doors shut, you numbskull!"

"Why?"

"Fun."

They place themselves around him.

"Do you dare?"

"Dare," says Herman.

He goes with them along the streetcar tracks. They turn around the corner and walk a ways down Oscars Street.

"Here," whispers Glenn.

Everyone stops and looks around. No one in sight. Then they run into the stairway entrance. Bjørnar holds watch at the bottom while Glenn, Karsten and Herman sneak up to the second floor. There is only one door there, and on the name plate it says Hulda Hansen. There's a newspaper on the doormat. Hulda Hansen is most certainly not at home, Herman thinks.

Glenn fastens the noose around the door handle. Karsten tightens and ties the clothesline to the banister with six granny knots. Then they look at Herman.

"You ring," Glenn whispers.

"What shall I say?"

"You meathead! She won't get the door open. That's the joke."

Herman goes closer, stops, looks at the others.

"Hurry up!"

He lifts his hand, makes a fist, sticks out his index finger and presses it on the doorbell. Three out-of-tune tones ring inside the apartment. Glenn and Karsten walk backwards toward the stairs. Nothing happens.

"Ring again!"

Herman rings again. And then he hears steps approaching the door, slow feet that shuffle over the floor. And he hears something else too. It sounds like crutches thumping out of rhythm between each step. And he sees the door handle pushed down.

"Someone's coming!" hisses Bjørnar from the first floor. "Someone's coming!"

Glenn and Karsten storm down the stairs. Herman remains standing and watches someone pull and tug at the door wanting out. The clothesline strains, but the knot on the banister just gets tighter and tighter.

"Get outta there, you idiot!" Glenn calls, and Herman hears them running out.

Hulda Hansen doesn't get the door open. She begins to shout. Herman tries to loosen the noose on the door handle, but it doesn't want to come off. Something warm and wet suddenly runs down his leg, and then two men come storming up the stairs, the manager and a policeman in uniform.

"Finally caught you red-handed, you rascal!" yells the

policeman, maneuvering Herman against the wall.

"Take it easy now, Miss Hansen! We'll get you free soon!"

The manager takes out pruning shears and clips the clothesline. Then the door opens, and Hulda Hansen leans on crutches peeking out. She looks at Herman. Herman looks at her. It's the Lady with the Fleas.

"We've caught your tormentor now. He'll pay for it!"

The Lady with the Fleas continues looking at Herman. Herman's eyes move to the policeman's shiny buttons. He can feel it running down in his right boot.

"It isn't him," she says.

"It isn't him?"

The manager is confused and the policeman loosens his grip.

"I know him. He usually brings me the newspaper."

She isn't able to bend down to the mat. The guard picks up the paper for her and has restless eyes.

"I see. Is that the way it is."

He turns suddenly toward Herman.

"Well, boy. Did you see anyone when you came?"

Herman swallows and swallows. There must be a worm in his Adam's apple. The policeman straightens his jacket and walks away a few steps while he turns up his nose.

"Saw two people running up Oscars Street."

"Did you recognize them?"

"Just saw them from behind."

"Were they your age?"

"A little older, I think. Maybe thirty."

The manager looks discouragingly at the policeman.

"Well, let's go look for them!"

Then they stomp down the stairs again, but Herman stands in the same spot and doesn't move as it runs out of his pant leg. The Lady with the Fleas looks at him a long time, her body twitching a little.

"Coming in?" she asks. "As long as you're here."

"Okay," says Herman, lifts his boot and walks with a stiff leg after her.

It's dark in her place too, so dark that he almost has to

feel his way forward with his hands. Suddenly she lights a chandelier, and he sees that the living room is full of sofas, and the walls are covered with photographs. From the ceiling hang long cords, one after another, with handles at the bottom, almost like the Frogner streetcar. The curtains are closed at all the windows.

Hulda Hansen sits down slowly on one of the sofas, rests her body and turns toward Herman who is staring at the ceiling.

"I use them sometimes when I can't find my crutches."

"That's clever," says Herman.

"The manager hung them up for me."

Herman says nothing to that.

"You can sit down if you like."

"I'm just fine right here."

"Why did you tie my door shut?"

Herman takes a step away from the chandelier and places himself in the shadow along the wall.

"Didn't know that you lived right here," he says softly.

"But the others knew, perhaps?"

"I've never done it before," Herman whispers and is ashamed from his face down to his stomach.

"Will you ask them to quit?"

"Shall do what I can."

"Then we won't talk about it anymore."

But Herman doesn't know what else they can talk about. He looks at the door. It's a long way there. If he runs now, he'll be out in two shakes, and then he can keep running to the end of the Earth and take the boat from there.

He doesn't run.

"You aren't afraid of me any longer?" Hulda Hansen asks, holding her hands around her body.

"Would you like a chestnut?"

Herman lays one of them on a table before she answers.

"I used to eat chestnuts," she says.

"You ate chestnuts?"

"Roasted chestnuts. In Rome."

"Have you been to Rome?"

"I've been almost everywhere. Your name is Herman, isn't it?"

"Have you been to Adapazari too?"

"That's one of the few places I haven't been."

She struggles a while with rising, climbs along the ropes and comes back with a glass of juice for Herman and a box of King Haakon candies.

"Did you have a little accident out in the hall?"

"Just in one pant leg."

She sits down and is silent while they each eat a candy. Then Herman can no longer hold back.

"How did the fleas get on you?" he asks quickly.

Herman doesn't quite know whether she's smiling or if she's getting angry. For safety's sake, he moves farther into the corner. But then she begins to laugh, and he takes a step forward again. Then she stops laughing.

"I don't have fleas on me. It's just something you all call me. The Lady with the Fleas. Because I walk so funny."

"I didn't really believe it anyway."

"I have something called Saint Vitus Dance."

Herman thinks about it.

"It's a strange dance," he says quietly.

"It's a kind of illness. But I used to dance. I was an actress. A movie actress."

Her face gets a little strange. She lifts her arm, looks like it hurts, and manages at last to point at one of the photographs.

Herman goes closer and looks at it. A lady with a tight skirt, much too small earmuffs, boyish hair and a long cigarette in the corner of her mouth sits on a car hood with her legs crossed.

"Was that you?"

"That was me. Right before I became famous. And long before I became sick."

Then Herman eyes another photograph. He keeps quiet and stares a long time. It's a man without hair. He doesn't have a single hair on his entire head, and he doesn't even have a cap. He just stands there in a black shirt, looking straight ahead as if nothing was happening.

"That's Yul Brynner," says Hulda Hansen.

"But who *is* he?" Herman asks.

"A famous actor. I played opposite him in a film once. It was called *The King and I.*"

"Were you the queen?"

"That I was. I was the queen."

"But the king must have had hair then?"

"He was as you see him there."

"Did you really like him?"

"Of everyone I have played opposite, he is my favorite."

Herman has to look back at the picture of Yul Brynner again. Then he turns to Hulda Hansen.

"Have you played opposite the Hunchback of Notre Dame too?"

She looks away and eats another candy.

"Shouldn't I have asked that?" Herman asks softly.

He sets down the juice glass and walks slowly toward the door.

"I don't feel sorry for you, Hulda Hansen!" he says suddenly loudly.

Now she looks at him again and smiles what she can.

"Will you visit me another day?"

"Might well happen," says Herman.

When he comes come, Mother is waiting for him. She sits in the kitchen with even more coffee and has something she wants to say.

"Where have you been, Herman?"

"Not at the schoolyard," he says quickly.

She looks at him over the coffee cup.

"Do you want supper?"

"Think I'll go right to my room and study."

"That's certainly wise. Barrel told me about your Christmas exam, by the way."

Herman tries to hide his leg under the table.

"I didn't like all of your story," Mother continues.

"That was how it goes. Barrel read it wrong."
Mother is silent while she pours a new cup.
"Where is Father?" Herman asks.
"He's out with the boys. They finished the building today."
"He's quite good, I must say."
"And Herman, it's not good to take away when you should add. Think what would happen if I did that at the store?"
"Then Jacobsen Jr. would become poor and have to go to the Salvation Army."
"Exactly. Are you using that old cap again now?"
"Think so."
Mother sighs, but suddenly she has more to say.
"Someone broke a window at the school when we were at the parents' meeting."
Herman curls his toes in his wet sock.
"Broke a window?"
"With a huge rock?"
"A rock?"
He ponders it.
"Did you see them?"
"How many were there, Herman?"
Mother puts down the cup and looks at him. Herman slowly sinks down on a chair and his thigh itches, it itches along his entire leg and he can't sit still.
"What have you done with your pants?" Mother asks.
Herman is relieved.
"Let me tell you. On Balders Street there came a German shepherd, and it was bigger than a camel and ran after me."
"It didn't bite you, did it?"
"Let me tell you more. It peed on me instead because there were no lampposts there."
"I'd better wash them then."
He pulls them off right there, runs to the bathroom and washes in shampoo. Later, he gets to be in peace in his room. He sits by the globe, thinking. He thinks of the queen who got sick from dancing too much. He thinks about the bald king and the king's gardener who became wet in the head. That's what he should have asked: if Hulda Hansen knew the

Bottle Man. He should have asked if she knew Grandfather too. Then he thinks of something else. He draws his breath so deep that he almost can't get it out again. Have I shamed Zorro now? he wonders. Have I done great shame to Zorro? He lays down to sleep thinking that at least he didn't have the secret costume on so no one could think it was Zorro who broke the window and tied shut the door of Hulda Hansen. It was no double. It was Herman Fulkt who did it.

At the same time the front bell rings. Father must have lost the key because he was out with Bock and Rags. But suddenly Mother is at the door.

"There's a visitor for you," she says.

She smiles in a sly manner that cannot bode well.

"Say I have a roast in the oven," whispers Herman.

Mother takes a step to the side and Ruby comes in. She closes the door behind her and looks at Herman.

"Are you going to bed so early?" she asks.

"Haven't gotten up yet."

She sits on the only chair and looks around.

"Real nice room you have."

"Dad built it."

They don't say anything more for at least five minutes. Herman wonders whether he should put on the Zorro costume over his pajamas anyway, but he doesn't.

"Aren't you skating anymore?" Ruby asks.

"The season is over."

He stares at her hair. He has never seen it so red. He almost can't stand to look at it for very long. She does a little toss with her head, and Herman looks out the window instead. There he can see her reflection.

"I came in fifth," Ruby says.

Herman has nothing to say to that.

"You were pretty good yourself, too."

"Was I?"

"You almost beat me."

"I forgot to polish my skates before the start."

"And you were hurt."

Herman must think it over.

"That I was. In my right or left knee."

"And there was bad ice on the inside."

"Yes indeed. I really had to go twice outside."

They don't say anything for awhile. When it's over, Ruby is the first to speak. She speaks lowly.

"Have you lost all your hair now, Herman?"

"Not altogether."

He turns the globe, and America travels by. Ruby comes closer.

"May I see?"

"Why?"

"I've never seen it before."

Herman slowly pulls off the cap and bends his head. He can't hear if Ruby says anything.

"Are you afraid now?" he whispers.

Then he feels a hand, a hand touching his skull, finger by finger, and carefully stroking the last hairs that hang at the neck.

"Don't say anything at school tomorrow," he whispers even lower.

"We won't let on anything."

He puts on the cap again and looks at the globe which continues to spin. He stops it.

"Do you live out at Majorstua?" Herman asks.

"You can come over some day," Ruby says.

23.

HERMAN WAKES UP EARLY. He wakes so early that he can only remember having closed one eye. A lot has happened lately, he says to himself, getting up. The pants hang over the chair and are dry. He sneaks to the bathroom and back. He takes off the cap, pulls out the bottom drawer and takes out the wig. He sets in on his head, feels around and feels almost nothing. He tries standing on his hands. It doesn't fall off. He bends out the window. It doesn't blow away. Then he packs his school bag and takes a trip to the kitchen. He wasn't the first one in the world, it turns out. There sits Mother, still drinking coffee. Her eyes are so tired that they hang by a thin thread.

"Are you up already, Herman?"

"Thanks the same."

He opens the refrigerator and drinks milk right out of the bottle.

"Where's father?" he asks.

"He hasn't gotten home yet."

"He isn't gone for good?"

"He'll come when he thaws."

"Then he'll surely come soon."

Only then does Mother discover the wig. An astonished smile wakes her face.

"I don't believe it! I see a wig!"

"Is it on the right way? I don't want to have the forelock at the neck."

She straightens it a little and must take another good look at him.

"Wish I had one like that myself! Then I wouldn't have to get permanents at Fats."

"Maybe you can borrow it some Saturday. But I'd better go now."

Outside the gate at Harelabben stand Glenn, Karsten and Bjørnar. They come running towards him, and Glenn gets in front.

"Did you tell?"

"I didn't tell," says Herman.

They look at his wig but don't do anything with it.

"So you didn't tell?"

"No, and that's final."

"Good goin', Herman."

"But don't tie her door shut anymore. Otherwise there'll be trouble."

"Did they say that?" Glenn asks.

"I say that," says Herman.

Fortunately the bell rings right then.

Barrel is sitting behind the teacher's desk, breathing heavily, and has to use two chairs to have enough room. Every time someone stares too long at the wig, he hits the floor with the pointer. Only Ruby pretends not to notice. She pretends a little too much. On the board Barrel has drawn fourteen different timber cruisers and written in green chalk: *Forests and forest use in Norway.* Herman notes in his work book: *Furniture is made from fine wood. Teak is not a Norwegian tree. In children's rooms, one uses pine furniture. Dining room furniture of birch is beautiful. Oak is also made into fine furniture. School desks are made of spruce.*

Then the door opens. The principal takes two steps into the room, turns on his heel, and everyone has stood up. Barrel almost falls between the two chairs, but gets to his feet eventually while the principal aims his eyes like two cannons from desk to desk, skipping the girls.

"Serious incidents have taken place!" he shouts. "A window is broken in my office! It was broken last night and the culprit was seen!"

Herman has problems with his balance. It is exactly like being in the middle of the turn at Frogner Stadium. He has to steer with one hand and support himself on the desk with the other in order not to swerve out into the next row.

"I order the guilty party to report at once and make the suffering short! Who was it!"

Not even the wig can help me now, thinks Herman. Now I have to go to prison for seven years bad luck and repeat just as many years and be the world's biggest dwarf.

He is about to raise his hand. Then something happens behind him.

"Me," says Glenn, standing with his arm in the air.

"It was me," says Karsten, waving his hand.

"Me too!" says Bjørnar with both arms over his head.

"I thought so!" shouts the principal, turning toward Barrel. "I thought so! Forward march!"

Barrel is a little confused and slumps down on the chairs, which creak awfully, while Glenn, Karsten and Bjørnar walk in rhythm out of the classroom.

The rest of the hour Herman uses to draw a timber-marking hammer in three colors. Then he writes: *The log must go to a saw mill or pulp mill. The paper factory must also have lots of trees. The timber goes to the mill. There it is sawed up into boards. Some of the timber goes to pulp mills and paper factories. All paper we write on has been timber.*

When the bell rings, Ruby looks at him quickly and doesn't let on.

Herman waits at the gate at Harelabben awhile. But Glenn, Karsten and Bjørnar don't come. Egg does instead. He stops in front of Herman and looks down at the wig.

"You standing here?" he asks.

"As one can see."

"They won't show up for awhile yet. They're copying the words to 'Now the Groves Revive' fifteen times each in handwriting. It takes awhile."

Egg looks up the street, but stays put.

"Nice wig you have," he says.

"It's not a wig. It's real human hair."

Egg rubs his chin a long time.

"Say, Herman, do you know why you all call me Egg?"

"Should like to know."

"Me too," says Egg. "Anyway, I was Norwegian champion in vaulting. In 1953."

He is quiet awhile. Then he livens up.

"Yes, yes. But I guess I don't need to know why they call Woody Woody?"

"Just ask," says Herman.

Egg doesn't. He just laughs loudly and wanders down the sidewalk. Herman watches him. Suddenly the cleaning lady pops up at the corner, and they walk together past the church. Egg and egg white! Herman shouts at them, but they don't hear. Then Woody comes too. He takes long steps in his course across the schoolyard, looking every which way and talking loudly to no one but himself.

Then Herman runs the other way. He runs to the construction site at Vika.

It looks as if the building is holding up the sky. And it is almost entirely of glass, transparent, and the sun, hanging by a thread over Oslo Fjord, fills it with light, and the whole building shines so bright that Herman has to look away before he has seen enough.

Then he sees the crane.

He finds a barracks behind a tall wooden fence that is being torn down. He knocks on the door, and it opens all by itself. He peeks in. There are two men in blue overalls at a table looking each other in the eyes. One has a beard on half his face, and the other is sunburned all over his face.

Herman clears his throat. They don't hear. He goes out and knocks again.

"Come in, damn it!" says a voice.

"But if it's the foreman, get out!" says a second voice.

They laugh at that a long time. When they're done, Herman opens the door, and they turn to him at the same time.

"It isn't the foreman," says the man with the beard.

"And he's lucky he's not," says the second one.

"He's very lucky!" says a third voice, which Herman has heard before.

On a narrow bench under the window lies Father with a towel over his head.

"You must be Herman!" the sunburned man suddenly shouts.

Father rises immediately, his face staring out confused, and gets his sight collected.

"Herman? Hi, Herman. What are you doing here?"

But before Herman can answer, the two men are up from their chairs extending huge hands with hair and band-aids on them.

"Bock here! Pleased to meet you!"

"And this is Rags! Or vice-versa. Herman, did you see it? Did you *see* that eel!"

Herman peeks over at Father who doesn't quite know what to do.

"Just barely," says Herman.

"It must have been huge! A meter? Do you think it was a meter?"

"Maybe one and a half. There was more under water than I saw."

"You'll have to come with us sometime, Herman! Have I told you about the one I got in '59? Have you heard about the Loch Ness monster? Well, it's just an earthworm compared to the one I got in '59 at Fred Olsen Wharf. Do you know what I did with the skin?"

Now Father is up too.

"Herman, this is quite a surprise. Was there something you wanted?"

"He wanted to meet us!" shouts Bock.

"I thought maybe I could go up in the crane," Herman says lowly. "Anyway, I have my wig on."

"It's an honor to be able to loan you my helmet!" Bock and Rags say in chorus.

Herman climbs first, inside the four-sided ladder, counting the steps inside. They are rough so he won't slip on them. He has come to thirty-two and begins counting over again. Under him climbs Father. Herman feels he'll soon get dizzy when the people on the ground are as small as gumdrop men in every color, when the wind makes the crane sway, when the city suddenly stands on edge and the sky hangs vertically an arm's length away from him, and he doesn't know which direction he is climbing.

"Don't look down!" Father shouts. "We'll be up soon!"

Herman closes his eyes. The helmet is heavy on his head. He moves his hands and feet step by step, and everything quivers, like in a dream. He must open his eyes again to see if he really is there. He is there, on the way up the crane, and he sees the planet spinning around at a tremendous speed while a sea gull to the left sits still in the wind. Then Father comes up next to him, grabs around his waist with one arm and opens the cabin door with the other. They crawl in, and Herman has to sit down awhile until everything comes to rest. Then he takes off the helmet and feels whether the wig is there too.

"The finest hair I've ever seen!" says Father.

Herman doesn't quite know what he means. He stands next to him and knows what he meant. The ship to America glides out Oslo Fjord with two yellow smokestacks, past Nesodden, where the snow has begun to melt at the wall of the house. Behind Frogner Park they can see the cemetery where Grandfather lies in a bed of earth now. And around the city stands the Norwegian forest tight and green with white lakes here and there. Then Herman suddenly catches sight of Glenn, Karsten and Bjørnar. They're coming out of the schoolyard with swollen thumbs and cauliflower ears, and Barrel stands at the classroom window trying to make a tassel from a bunch of yarn in three different colors. By Bislett, Egg and the cleaning lady walk arm in arm, and Woody sneaks behind them. Hulda Hansen is on her way to the Beauty Salon, and on Bygdøy Avenue, Fats opens the door for his old Mother and lets her in. At Majorstua, the doctor and nurse go up the stairs in knickers with skis on their backs.

And down Kirke Road comes Ruby at full speed, with a blue newspaper cart behind her and a huge bunch of keys in the hand she has drawn an H on.

"The line to that eel didn't really break," says Herman.

"Isn't it great! Like to live up here!"

Father throws out his arms.

"I broke it myself."

"Do you see the boat to Nesodden? There! That's the *Prince* for sure. I can see all the way from here!"

Herman sees that it isn't the *Prince,* but doesn't tell Father.

"Why are you angry with the foreman?" he asks instead.

Father rubs his eyes.

"He docked us an hour's pay this morning, you see."

"I've saved some for hard times," says Herman. "Two crowns and seventy-eight *øre.* But it's really Mother's."

Father lays his arm on his shoulders.

"Is Mother angry?"

"So-so."

The wind takes hold of the crane and they have to hold tight.

"Think I have depth perception too," says Herman.

Then they see that the ship to America will soon be past the world's end and the yellow smokestacks disappear downhill.

"Maybe we should go home now, Dad?"

SPRING

24.

HERMAN STANDS IN THE MIDDLE of the wide room. It is dark in all directions. He can only glimpse the outline of the wicker chairs, the radio cabinet, the table with the oil cloth, the door to the porch that he closed behind him, and the windows that are still nailed shut. But he senses all the smells, stronger than ever, of old magazines that he will soon read again, dry kelp that will crumble between his fingers without him even coming near, and the apples from last year that they left. The sun has warmed up the house for several days; he boils a little under the wig and has to wipe his neck.

Then a bright stripe appears at one of the windows. Mother and Father lift off the first shutter, and the insects on the sill waken to life, butt against the windowpane and buzz confusedly. And that's how Herman sees the room he's standing in slowly but surely fill with light, and at last his parents open the door to the porch and Father leans on Mother, or maybe the other way around.

"That's that," says Herman.

He stands out on the deck on the way back to the city. The fjord is full of white sails that hang in the sun. The sweat oozes from the wig and stings his eyes. He has to move over to the shade by the hawser awhile. Then he discovers that the boat is called *Flaskebekk,* and he remembers Grandfather's story, which he never forgets. That was pretty lucky, Herman thinks, that they got *Flaskebekk* up from the Indian Ocean with man and mouse and sailed it back to Pier B. He runs through the lounge and finds his parents in the back, each with ice cream running over their fingers.

"When is a sailor not a sailor?" he asks quickly.

"Maybe when he's seasick," Father tries.

"When he's aboard!"

Mother laughs so loud that *Flaskebekk* has to go backwards the last bit, but fortunately the clock on the City Hall tower doesn't stop. It is a quarter after four, a Sunday in May, 1962.

When they get home, they have to open all the windows there too. A marching band is practicing on another block and is almost drowned out by bicycle bells. Father is already in the bathroom scouring his hands and picking flakes off his shoulders.

"Guess what we're having for dinner?" Mother asks.

"Bishfalls," Herman suggests.

"No, and that's final."

"Stishficks with cream?"

"Hot dogs and fries! We have to practice too, don't we?"

"The record is eighteen with ketchup," Herman informs.

He goes to his room and stands at the window a long time. He turns the globe and sweats at the top of the head. The band is coming closer and playing a familiar song. There is something Herman has to think about. He has heard that some people have time ahead of them. He looks closely but can't see it. He turns. It isn't behind him either. Time must have lost it's tooth, Herman thinks. But then he sees something anyway; the buds on the trees on the other side of the street. The stubborn buds go absolutely to pieces, and out fold green leaves which finally cover the whole sky. That's incredible, thinks Herman.

He pulls out the bottom drawer, looks awhile at the skating cap lying there. He takes out the herbarium instead, and finishes it. He glues the back tight and lays it to dry on the window sill. If I don't find a white anemone this year, then I'll have to do without an enemy, thinks Herman.

Then he sneaks into his parent's bedroom. Their pajamas

lie helter skelter and Father has left behind two different socks in Mother's bed. He sits down at the three section mirror and looks.

"You and you!" he says loudly. "And Grandfather is Grandfather even if he is dead!"

He thinks awhile.

"And Herman is Herman and no other! That I promise."

He lifts the wig off and looks in the mirror again. He sees his skull from all angles. It is big and shiny and almost glows. He puts both hands on his own skull. It's smooth and good to the touch, not so much as a bump.

"Herman is Herman," he repeats. "I promise."

Then he runs out, slides down the banister and sprints right out in the street. His parents stand in the window and watch him, but he doesn't have time for them now. Another window also opens, and the Bottle Man leans out. The Bottle Man has come back and has filled out in the face and is dry behind the ears.

"*Tusan,* how fine you look!"

The Bottle Man almost has his feet on the sill.

"Look, Herman! *Titta!* They're playing for us!"

The band turns onto the street at full volume. All the heads turn simultaneously, and there are out-of-tempo snare drums for awhile and loud notes from the clarinets. Then they pass, with all the bicycles in tow.

Herman walks on. He doesn't know exactly where he's going. So he continues walking.

ALOPECIA AREATA: THE DISEASE OF HERMAN

Alopecia areata is a common disease that results in the loss of hair on the scalp and elsewhere and may have a profound effect on the quality of life of those affected. It appears without warning and usually starts with small, round, bare patches. Young persons are affected most often, but it can occur in males and females of any age. Although medically benign, its precipitous onset, recurrent episodes and unpredictable course disrupt many lives. At present there is no cure for alopecia areata although the hair may regrow by itself. There are treatments which are most effective in milder cases, but none are universally effective.

The National Alopecia Areata Foundation (NAAF) was formed in 1981 by a young Californian who had the disease and wanted to help others with alopecia areata. Picture what it would be like to be five years old and bald. Try to see alopecia areata through the eyes of parents like Herman's who watch their child's hair fall out day by day in patches.

In ten years, the Foundation has become the world center for alopecia areata, providing crucial support for patients, building public awareness, and helping foster research about the cause of the disease and treatments to reverse its course. The NAAF is the principal organization in the world funding and promoting research in alopecia areata—currently all from private funds. The Foundation is laying the groundwork for the future understanding of alopecia areata and has funded over $500,000 for research in the past five years.

For information about the National Alopecia Areata Foundation, write the foundation at P.O. Box 150760, San Rafael, California 94915-0760.

The typeface used throughout this book is Veljovic. It was typeset by Bets, Ltd. in Ithaca, New York and printed on acid-free paper by Thomson-Shore, Dexter, Michigan.